"Easily the craziest, weirdest, strangest, funniest, most obscene writer in America."
—*GOTHIC MAGAZINE*

"Carlton Mellick III has the craziest book titles... and the kinkiest fans!"
—CHRISTOPHER MOORE, author of *The Stupidest Angel*

"If you haven't read Mellick you're not nearly perverse enough for the twenty first century."
—JACK KETCHUM, author of *The Girl Next Door*

"Carlton Mellick III is one of bizarro fiction's most talented practitioners, a virtuoso of the surreal, science fictional tale."
—CORY DOCTOROW, author of *Little Brother*

"Bizarre, twisted, and emotionally raw—Carlton Mellick's fiction is the literary equivalent of putting your brain in a blender."
—BRIAN KEENE, author of *The Rising*

"Carlton Mellick III exemplifies the intelligence and wit that lurks between its lurid covers. In a genre where crude titles are an art in themselves, Mellick is a true artist."
—*THE GUARDIAN*

"Just as Pop had Andy Warhol and Dada Tristan Tzara, the bizarro movement has its very own P. T. Barnum-type practitioner. He's the mutton-chopped author of such books as *Electric Jesus Corpse* and *The Menstruating Mall*, the illustrator, editor, and instructor of all things bizarro, and his name is Carlton Mellick III."
—*DETAILS MAGAZINE*

Also by
Carlton Mellick III

Satan Burger
Electric Jesus Corpse (Fan Club Exclusive)
Sunset With a Beard (stories)
Razor Wire Pubic Hair
Teeth and Tongue Landscape
The Steel Breakfast Era
The Baby Jesus Butt Plug
Fishy-fleshed
The Menstruating Mall
Ocean of Lard (with Kevin L. Donihe)
Punk Land
Sex and Death in Television Town
Sea of the Patchwork Cats
The Haunted Vagina
Cancer-cute (Fan Club Exclusive)
War Slut
Sausagey Santa
Ugly Heaven
Adolf in Wonderland
Ultra Fuckers
Cybernetrix
The Egg Man
Apeshit
The Faggiest Vampire
The Cannibals of Candyland
Warrior Wolf Women of the Wasteland
The Kobold Wizard's Dildo of Enlightenment +2
Zombies and Shit
Crab Town

The Morbidly Obese Ninja
Barbarian Beast Bitches of the Badlands
Fantastic Orgy (stories)
I Knocked Up Satan's Daughter
Armadillo Fists
The Handsome Squirm
Tumor Fruit
Kill Ball
Cuddly Holocaust
Hammer Wives (stories)
Village of the Mermaids
Quicksand House
Clusterfuck
Hungry Bug
Tick People
Sweet Story
As She Stabbed Me Gently in the Face
ClownFellas: Tales of the Bozo Family
Bio Melt
Every Time We Meet at the Dairy Queen,
Your Whole Fucking Face Explodes
The Terrible Thing That Happens
Exercise Bike
Spider Bunny
The Big Meat
Parasite Milk
Stacking Doll
Neverday
The Boy with the Chainsaw Heart
Mouse Trap
Snuggle Club
The Bad Box
Full Metal Octopus

GOBLINS
ON THE OTHER
SIDE

CARLTON MELLICK III

ERASERHEAD PRESS
PORTLAND, OREGON

ERASERHEAD PRESS
P.O. BOX 10065
PORTLAND, OR 97296

WWW.ERASERHEADPRESS.COM

ISBN: 978-1-62105-320-0

AUTHOR'S NOTE

I love reading short stories. I grew up on short stories. Ray Bradbury was my favorite author when I was a kid and I read every single short story of his that I could find. I still read the stories published in *Asimov's*, *Weird Tales*, and *Fantasy and Science Fiction* whenever I get the chance.

But, although I love works in the short form, I've never been much of a short story writer. I just don't like writing them. People ask me to write short stories for their magazines and anthologies all the time and I just have to kindly decline the invitation because I just can't do it. I'd much rather write novels and novellas. Compared to novels and novellas, short stories are limiting, they pay next to nothing, and they take almost the same amount of effort to write. I respect the hell out of people who do write short stories, but they just aren't for me.

There was a time when I used to write them regularly. When I was a kid, I wrote a lot of short stories. When I was first trying to break into publishing, I wrote even more. I strongly believed that writing short stories was the only way to start a writing career and get noticed by readers and publishers. I had notebooks upon notebooks of short story ideas that I hoped to one day flesh out into bite-sized tales. But at some point, about a decade ago, I just stopped. I gave up. And I don't see myself returning to them any time soon.

I still come up with ideas for short stories from time to time. I still think about how I can compact a narrative into a small 5,000 word package. But I never write them as I originally imagined they would be. Instead, I take my short story ideas and flesh them out into novella-lengthed works that can be published as stand-alone books. *The Terrible Thing That Happens*, *Sweet Story*, *I Knocked Up Satan's Daughter*, *As She Stabbed Me Gently in the Face*, *Exercise Bike*, *Parasite Milk*, *Spider Bunny*, and *Every Time We Meet at the Dairy Queen Your Whole Fucking Face Explodes* were all originally short story ideas that were fleshed out into longer books.

Goblins on the Other Side is another of these books that was originally supposed to be a short story. But this one didn't come from just any short story idea. This book was based on the very first short story idea I've ever had. It's something I came up with as a kid, long before I was ever published. It's a story I have wanted to write for a very long time and have finally gotten around to finishing almost thirty years later.

Taking ideas I had when I was a kid and actually writing them out is not something I've ever done before. And there's a good reason why I've never done this. I came up with a lot of dumb ideas back then. Some of them are so embarrassingly bad that I will never talk about them no matter how drunk someone gets me at a bar. But this is one that has always stuck with me, even after all these years. Think of it as kind of a collaboration between myself and the child version of myself. It's like if I had a time machine and adult-me and kid-me pulled an *Axe Cop* or something.

So here it is, my sixty-third book. I hope you enjoy my childhood brain.

—Carlton Mellick III, 12/17/2021 6:52am

For Goblin

CHAPTER
ONE

Nora doesn't want to go to Heaven today. She'd much rather stay at home and cut mohawks into her Barbie dolls, stomp on Lego houses like an angry kaiju, or use a lighter to melt all her crayons into an ugly multi-colored blob. There's nothing more boring than going on a trip with her family. Her stupid little brother always pesters her to play robots vs pirates with him. Her stupid parents never let her draw vampires on her cell phone painting app. She's nine years old now. She doesn't know why she can't just stay at home by herself and do whatever she wants to do.

"Come on, get ready," her mother tells her, standing in her bedroom doorway with that annoyed look that's always on her face. "We're going to be late."

"I *am* getting ready," Nora says, sitting on the floor in her pajamas while painting tattoos on a green-haired Barbie doll.

Her mother goes to her and pulls the doll out of her hands. "Stop destroying your toys and put your clothes on."

Nora scowls at her mother and says, "I'm not destroying it. I'm giving her a new look."

Her mother stuffs the doll in a box on the highest shelf in her closet and says, "We're leaving in fifteen minutes."

Nora just sulks in her room until her mother yells at her again. Then she puts on a blood-red tank top and some camouflage shorts she got from the Goodwill. But once she's all ready to go, her mother still yells at her for not wearing the clothes she picked out for her.

"You can't wear that," her mother cries. "Put on the pants and cardigan like I told you to."

"But it's too hot for sweaters," Nora whines.

"It's going to be cold in Heaven. You'll freeze to death in that outfit."

Her mother takes her to her room and forces her to change into warmer clothing, not leaving her alone for even a second until she's ready to go to the afterlife.

Nora doesn't understand why it's so important for them to go to Heaven to visit grandma. She only died a few weeks ago. That's hardly enough time for them to even miss her. It's not like they'll never see her again. She wishes they would've waited until summer was over so she could've at least missed a couple of days of school. Visiting dead loved ones in the afterlife is an even better excuse than pretending to be sick. The teachers let you take as much time as you need and don't even expect you to do homework until you get back home.

She already had to sit through a boring funeral with her bratty cousins and snobby aunts and uncles who kept apologizing for her loss like it even means anything to her. It was all a waste of time in her opinion, a waste of precious summer vacation days. She could've been riding bikes with her friends or playing Minecraft. She could've been swimming at her neighbor's pool party. And now she's going to waste more of her summer visiting grandma. They don't even have television or Wi-Fi in Heaven. It's going to be so lame.

On the car ride there, Nora can't contain her boredom. It's a four-hour drive and she's only able to play on her phone for twenty minutes before her mother takes it away, telling her that she has to spend time with her family instead of with her head in an electronic device. Although she's having the worst time, Nora's little brother Jack seems to love the idea of going to Heaven. To him, it's like they're going to an exciting amusement park like Disneyland or Magic Mountain, like this trip is the highlight of his summer. The whole way there he won't shut up about it.

He keeps asking questions like: "What's it like in Heaven, Mommy? Do people need to eat dinner there? What kind of food do they eat? Are there dogs there? Do dogs go to Heaven after they die? How about cars? Do they drive cars?"

Their mother just responds to every one of his questions with: "You'll see for yourself soon enough."

But then Jack asks a question that hits a nerve.

He asks, "What about Grandpa? Will Grandpa be there?"

When he says this, their parents go quiet for a moment. Their mother bites her lip. Their father tightens his grip on the steering wheel.

"Will I finally get to meet him?" Jack asks.

When their mother answers him, her voice is in a severe tone. She doesn't want to talk about her father.

"Your grandpa isn't in Heaven," she tells him.

"Why not?" Jack asks. "You said that we can visit anyone who died in Heaven."

Their mother doesn't want to explain more. She lets out a breath and tries to ignore her youngest child. Nora answers for her.

"Grandpa's in Hell, dumbass," she says.

Her mother glares at her daughter and tells her not to call her little brother names.

"Why is Grandpa in Hell?" Jack asks.

His mother sighs and says, "Because he was a very bad man, sweetheart."

"Can we go see him in Hell someday?"

Nora laughs at her brother's question. Her mother doesn't find it funny at all.

"We're not taking you to Hell, Jack," their father says in an overly loud tone, breaking his silence for the first time in over an hour. "It's too dangerous and expensive. Children under eighteen aren't allowed there anyway. Now shut up about Grandpa and let me drive in peace."

Jack sinks in his seat and pouts in response to his father's words. Nora thinks it's funny that her brother wants to visit their abusive grandfather in Hell. Even she wouldn't want to do something like that. She barely remembers her grandfather, but she knows exactly what an alcoholic jerk he was.

The gateway to Heaven is crowded when they get there. At least a hundred cars are lined up in six rows, waiting to traverse to the other side. They're so far back in the queue that they can barely see the swirling blue portal up ahead.

When they enter the line, Nora groans. "I thought we were finally there! How long is this going to take?"

Her father cleans his glasses with his polo shirt and says, "It'll take as long as it takes."

"Why is going to Heaven such a pain?" Nora whines.

"You're lucky you're even able to go to Heaven at all," her mother explains. "I had to wait twenty years before I was able to see my grandmother after she died. People didn't even know Heaven existed at all back then."

Nora doesn't care about what her mom has to say. She's sick of hearing about how good she has it compared to her parents when they were kids. So what if she has high-speed internet and cell phones and 4k televisions and technology that lets them go to the afterlife whenever they want? It's still annoying that they have to wait in such a long line. She'd much rather have stayed home and watched movies in bed all weekend.

The line goes much faster than anticipated, but Nora still complains about the wait. When they get to the front, everyone in the car stares at the bright glowing lights that emanate from the gateway. It's like a shimmering pool of magic, twinkling like fairy fire, issuing a faint noise that sounds like a thousand whispering spirits. But Nora isn't impressed. It looks kind of cool but nothing she hasn't seen before on television.

A man in a powder-blue security uniform steps up to the car and peeks through the driver's side window. He leans in, giving Nora a good look at his badly maintained reddish-brown mustache and bulging green eyes.

"Passports and tickets, please," the security guard says.

Nora's father hands him the documentation. While looking it over, the guard asks, "Is this your first time to Heaven?"

Her father nods his head. "My wife has gone a few times before, but it will be a first for the rest of us."

The guard checks some boxes on his form and then asks, "Are there any pets or animals in the car?"

"No, sir," the father says.

"Any produce or food of any kind, including juice or caloric beverages?"

"Nothing of the sort."

Nora holds her hand over her pocket, just in case anybody notices the bulge in her pants. She thinks it's a stupid rule that you can't bring food into Heaven, so she decided to smuggle in a bunch of candy bars with her. Food in the afterlife is supposed to be weird and gross. She's already a picky eater and isn't sure if she'll be capable of stomaching any of it. She'd much rather play it safe and bring along her own food to eat, even if all she can take is candy she stole from the cabinet above the refrigerator.

"Everyone has the appropriate masks and costumes, correct?" the guard asks.

"Yes, we've got them right here," the father says, holding up the costumes from the middle seat.

Nora doesn't like the look of the costumes. They're so ugly and weird, like they were taken from the skins of deformed monsters. She can't believe they have to wear such gross outfits while in Heaven.

The guard looks them over carefully and then nods his head. "Be sure to wear your masks at all times once you exit the vehicle. You can only take them off while inside your loved one's dwelling. This is for your own protection." He points to the backseat, looking specifically at Nora. "And keep an eye on the little ones. Don't let them wander."

After returning their passports, the guard gives them a small booklet that looks similar to a travel brochure for a state park or any other tourist attraction.

"Take this pamphlet," the guard says. "It will explain everything. Heaven is perfectly safe as long as you follow

CHAPTER TWO

When Nora opens her eyes, she finds herself in another world. They are driving down a country road, not much different than the ones back home but the asphalt is a bit darker and smoother. The sky is purple and full of pink clouds. The forest around them is dense with deep red and white trees and bushes. It's late autumn in Heaven. Violet leaves are piled on the ground along the side of the road, blowing in the chilly breeze.

Nora rubs her arms and pants, making sure all of the goo is gone. It felt so cold and gross. She's surprised it didn't leave a sticky residue all over her. When she looks back, she sees the blue gateway shrinking in the distance. Despite the dozens of other cars passing through the gateway, there aren't any other vehicles on the road with them. It's like they all exited the portal in different places than Nora's family did, coming out in completely different areas of Heaven. Since the afterlife is supposed to be endless, a hundred times larger than Earth and continuously growing with every person who dies, it makes sense that not everyone would travel to the same destination. It would probably take years to drive from one side of Heaven to the other.

"So what do you think?" Nora's mother asks, motioning toward the landscape around them. "It's beautiful, isn't it?"

Nora hates to admit that she agrees with her mother. Looking out the car window, she is amazed at how interesting the afterlife looks. Any videos or photos taken in Heaven don't turn out when they are brought back to the other side, so she's never seen any real footage of the afterlife. And even how Heaven is portrayed in paintings and movies doesn't do it justice. It's a dark and eerie landscape that feels like a place for witches and Halloween. It's way less lame than Nora was expecting.

There are tall skinny trees with red and tan stripes. Large white rose bushes with long black thorns. Hills of purple and red grass. Fields of pink dandelions and pale rocks piled up like bones on the side of the road. There aren't any houses or people or other cars. The only sign of civilization is the road they're driving on and an old stone wall that runs alongside the road, covered in red moss.

Jack has his hands and nose pressed tightly to the glass, staring out at the purple landscape.

"Where are all the people, Mommy?" Jack asks. "I don't see anyone."

Their mother says, "Heaven is a big place. Everyone lives far apart here."

"Are there any ice cream shops? I want to see what

ice cream in Heaven tastes like."

"There aren't any stores of any kind. Money doesn't exist here. There's no need for it."

"Where does Grandma live? Is her house very far?"

"We should be there soon," she says.

Jack squishes his nose so tight to the glass that he probably looks pig-faced on the other side. He sticks out his tongue and licks it side to side, snorting at the fields of red.

As they drive down the road at a casual speed, Nora notices something especially interesting. There're these tall black bushes growing flowers like she's never seen before. The flowers are bigger than a human head and shaped like purple tarantulas. They are the most beautiful flowers Nora has ever seen. She wonders if she'd be able to cut one and take it home with her. Or maybe get some seeds and grow them in her backyard.

Nora tries to look deeper into the woods to see if she can find more of the tarantula flowers, but there's a thick mist coming in, blocking her view of anything too far from the road. As they continue, the mist gets thicker, making it nearly impossible to spot the alien flower bushes even if they're in there somewhere. Without being able to see the stimulating scenery, Nora finds herself getting bored again.

But just before she turns away, she sees something in the mist. Not just one thing, but several of them. Shadowy figures are lurking in the woods. They're shaped like humans but just stand there, unmoving. As they go farther up the road, there are more and more shadows in the mist. Hundreds of them. Nora squints her eyes, trying to get a good look at them. But she can't make out any details of any of them. She has no idea who or what they are.

"There they are!" Jack cries, pointing at the figures in the mist. "There are all the people!"

When their mother looks out of the window and peers into the mist, she just shakes her head. "Those aren't people."

"Of course they are!" Jack says. "Look at them!"

Their mother reaches back and pulls Jack's face away from the glass. "They're nothing. Don't look at them. It's just Heaven noise."

"What's Heaven noise?" Nora asks.

Her mother answers, "There's a lot of noise in Heaven. Just ignore it and it will go away."

But this only intrigues Nora more. She digs for more information, but her mother won't explain any more than she has. Nora looks out the window, watching the figures in the mist. Some of them start moving, stepping toward the roadway. But none of them get close enough for her to get a good look. None of them seem to be able to leave the mist or step over the stone wall separating the street from the woods.

"They look spooky," Jack says.

"Super spooky," Nora agrees.

Nora pulls a Baby Ruth out of her pocket, unwraps it, and takes a bite. With her eyes still on the mist, she doesn't realize what she's eating. The flavor is putrid, the texture is like live crickets buried in animal fat.

"Ewww!" Nora cries, spitting the food from her mouth.

Her mother looks over at her and sees the candy bar in her hand. Her eyes widen into a panic.

"Is that what I think it is?" she screams.

Nora is too busy rubbing her tongue with the bottom of her shirt to reply to her mother.

"You brought food through the gateway? Are you insane?"

"Goddammit, Nora," her father yells at her. "What the hell's wrong with you?"

Her mother takes the candy bar out of her hand. "I told you it's against the rules to bring food through the gateway. All organic material is mutated during transformation. It doesn't belong in Heaven. It makes food disgusting at best, poisonous at worst."

Nora pulls the rest of the candy bars out of her pocket and sees them squirming and pulsing under the wrappers. Her mother takes them away from her and asks, "Is this all of it?"

When Nora nods, her mother tosses all of the candy out of the window.

"You're in trouble, young lady," her mother says.

"How was I supposed to know that would happen?"

Nora says. "You didn't tell me shit about why I can't bring food to Heaven."

"Language!" her mother yells.

Nora spits onto the car floor, still gagging on the flavor as her little brother laughs his ass off at her. "I never would have done it if you just told me that candy would taste like puke here."

"Just do what I say, at least until we're back home. This is serious. You have to follow the rules. You can't just break the rules or do whatever you want."

"Fine," Nora says.

Her mother stares at her intently, making sure she's completely understood.

"You hear me?" she asks.

"I get it," Nora says.

But Nora's far more pissed off about it than her parents are. If they would just explain why the rules are the rules, then she might actually choose to obey them.

They pass only a dozen or so houses as they take the country road deeper into Heaven. Some of them are fancy modern mansions, while others look so small and old, made completely of cobblestone or wood logs. Nora isn't sure anyone even lives in any of them. Most of the houses appear abandoned. There are no lights on inside, no sign of life whatsoever. They are almost haunting in the misty woods. Nora wonders if all of them are just more of Heaven's noise, like the shadows. She wonders if they are dwellings that people moved into after they died.

When they reach their grandmother's house, they pull their car into the driveway. It's a nice suburban home, like those built in the 1950s. A white picket fence surrounds a bright green perfectly-manicured front lawn. Yellow paneling on the front of the house with bright orange shingles on the roof. A hedge separates the driveway from the rest of the yard, split by a stone pathway that leads to the front door.

As they pull up, Nora's mother's eyes widen. A smile grows on her face.

"Oh my god," she says. "It looks just like my child-hood home."

Nora doesn't know what the big deal is. It's just a boring house. If this was her dwelling in Heaven, she would have chosen a much fancier house to live in. She'd choose a giant mansion or a gothic castle or maybe a cruise ship or the biggest treehouse anyone has ever seen. An old-fashioned suburban home is totally boring.

"I can't believe it." Tears well up in her mother's eyes. "They tore this house down years ago. I never thought I'd see it again." She looks more carefully. "It's in the middle of the woods instead of a suburban cul-de-sac, but other than that it's identical."

As Nora's father turns the car off and pulls the parking brake, the porch light comes on and the front door opens. When a young pretty woman runs out, waving her hands with a big smile on her face, Nora's mother can't contain her excitement.

"That's her!" Mother says. "Look at her. She's so young!"

Nora and Jack don't get it. The woman doesn't look anything like their grandma. She's half the age she was just a few weeks ago, wearing a blue old-fashioned dress and high heel shoes. Her hair is bright red instead of white, worn up in a fifties hairdo. The only thing resembling Nora's grandma is her big pointed nose and horn-rimmed glasses.

"Who's that?" Jack asks as the woman approaches the car.

"That's your grandma," his mother says.

Jack doesn't seem to be convinced. "No she's not." The smile that was permanently plastered on his face the whole trip suddenly fades away. He doesn't seem to like this new look of Grandma's one little bit.

"Put on your costumes before you leave the car," their father says.

He hands out the masks and uniforms that he purchased last week, handing Nora the ugliest and most bizarre one of them all. She doesn't even want to touch it, let alone wear the nasty thing. It has horns and creepy devilish patterns. It's going to make her look like a mad witch doctor.

"Hi, kids!" their grandma says outside the car window. "Welcome to Heaven!"

Nora is the last to put on her costume and mask and leave the car. She reluctantly lets the young version of her grandma give her a way-too-tight hug and kiss on the cheek of her mask, and then turns to her mom to complain. "Why do we have to wear these stupid things?"

Her mother pats her on the head. "It's what everyone wears in Heaven, sweetie. It's so that you'll blend in with the locals."

"What locals?" Nora asks. "Nobody's here but Grandma."

"It's a rule so you have to follow it."

Her grandmother gives her daughter a look after witnessing the exchange and asks, "Why are you lying to her, Claire? Just tell the girl the truth for Christ's sake."

Claire argues, "Like you didn't do the same when I was her age."

"I never lied to you unless it was to protect you from your father."

"You lied to me my whole life!"

As they get into a heated argument, the rest of the family backs away so that they can stay out of it. Claire gets so emotional around her mother that she's beginning to sound a lot like Nora whenever she gets into an argument with her. She seems to have a lot of pent-up frustration with her mother which must have come to the surface after she died. She's probably been waiting weeks to see her just so she could give her mom a piece of her mind.

When they finish bickering with each other, Claire pops the trunk to get their luggage, grumbling to herself as she tugs on an overly large suitcase. The grandma doesn't seem to be phased by their argument in the slightest and just smiles widely as she turns to the kids.

She comes to Nora and Jack and says, "Let's go inside and get you out of those ugly costumes. I've got a surprise for you."

Jack's eyes light up and he says, "Presents? You got us presents?"

He seems to have already gotten used to his grandma's new appearance.

"Is it Christmas or your birthday?" she asks.

Jack's voice goes quiet. "No."

"Then you don't get any presents."

Jack makes an exaggerated pouting face. "Awww…"

"But I made you cookies."

Jack's smile comes back. "Cookies!"

"And this is Heaven so you can eat as many as you want."

Nora and Jack sit at the kitchen counter in front of a mountain of steaming hot fresh-baked chocolate chip walnut cookies. Jack eats them three at a time. Nora is just happy to finally get the taste of that putrid candy bar out of her mouth. Their costumes are scattered on the floor, leaving them for their grandma to clean up.

"So there's no calories in these, right?" Nora's father asks, pointing at the plate of cookies.

"Nope," his mother-in-law tells him. "They're basically an illusion. You'll taste the flavor and feel the texture, even feel your hunger get satisfied, but you're not really eating anything. You can eat a hundred of them and not gain a single pound."

"In that case, I'll take five," he says, grabbing a handful of cookies from the plate.

The grandma smiles. "That's one of the benefits and dangers of visiting Heaven. You can't bring food in, and the food here has no nutritional value, so you're starving yourself no matter how much you eat."

"Fine by me," he says. "I could stand to lose a few pounds."

Listening in to the conversation, Nora realizes that's why her parents forced her to eat so much in the days leading up to their trip. They were trying to fatten her up knowing that she'd essentially be starved for three days straight. But as long as the food prevents hunger pangs, she won't notice much of a difference outside of a little fatigue here and there.

When Claire gets inside, she drops all the luggage and closes the door. She pulls off her mask and looks at the home she grew up in. Her attitude changes completely from what it was outside. Her eyes are wide and tearing. A bright smile is plastered on her face. She goes to the living room couch and touches it, just to make sure it's real. Then she goes to the fireplace mantle and looks at all the old, framed photographs from when she was a child. Everything in the room no longer exists on Earth. They all burned up in the fire many years ago.

Her mom goes to her and asks, "So what do you think?"

Claire just goes to her mother and gives her a hug.

"Oh Mom, it's so perfect," she says, wiping her tears away.

"I know," the grandma says. "I felt the same way when I first arrived."

Claire steps back to fully examine her mother in the body she was in when she was a child.

"You look great, Mom," she says.

The grandma spins in a circle to show off her body like a new outfit. "I *feel* great, too. I don't have back pains. I don't have the misery of those horrible chemo treatments. Part of me wishes I died years ago just to get my health back."

Claire hugs her mother again. "I missed you so much. I'm so happy we can be together again."

"I'm happy, too. I was so excited for you to come see the old place again. It's great that you're finally here."

"Have you seen Grandma yet?" Claire asks.

"Of course! Grandma and Grandpa come over to visit all the time. They're busy playing a tennis tournament this weekend so you won't be able to see them until your next trip, but they told me to send you their love. They can't wait to meet their great-grandchildren."

"What about the rest of your family? Your aunts and uncles? Have you seen them yet?"

Her mom shakes her head. "Not yet. Just Grandma,

Grandpa, and your Uncle Jeremy. There's a Miller family reunion coming up later in the year, so I'll see everyone then."

"Oh, that sounds great," Claire says. "Maybe we can come back to Heaven then so that the kids can meet everyone."

Her mom waves off her words. "No living people allowed, I'm afraid. You'll have to wait until after you die to attend."

Claire frowns but then shrugs it off. "Yeah, I guess there's a lot of places in Heaven that are off-limits to us visitors. At least it will give us something new to look forward to for after we die."

Grandma pats her shoulder and changes the subject. "You have to see your old room. It's exactly as it was when you were Nora's age."

Claire's eyes light up. "Seriously? Is my old doll collection in there?"

"It sure is," Grandma says, leading her down the hallway.

"Oh my god! I want to play with them right now!"

Nora rolls her eyes at her mom when she leaves the room. She can't believe how immature she's been acting since she arrived at her grandma's house. Who cares about this dumb old house anyway? It's not even half the size as the one they live in back home. When Nora's an adult she knows that she won't give two shits about visiting her childhood home if it gets rematerialized in Heaven. She'd much rather see something bigger and more fantastical, something that could never exist anywhere on Earth. Just living in your memories sounds boring to her. It would be a complete waste of her eternal paradise.

At dinnertime, they have a grand feast like nothing Nora has ever seen before. It's like an all-you-can-eat buffet. There's prime rib, roast duck, a Thanksgiving turkey, a Christmas ham, a pile of German sausages, walnut stuffing, mashed potatoes, macaroni casserole, grilled asparagus, braised red cabbage, dumplings, hushpuppies, and twelve different pies for dessert. Anything they want, they just ask Grandma for it, and she opens the oven or the fridge and instantly pulls out a fully cooked platter of food like magic.

Nora's parents are pigging out like crazy people, shoveling the delicious meal into their gullets like they haven't eaten in weeks. They have serving after serving, each one a full meal in itself. Jack, on the other hand, goes right for the dessert. He eats a big slice of every kind of pie except for the mincemeat. Then he orders a banana split, a box of doughnuts, fifteen different chocolate bars, and a bunch of Twinkies for some reason even though he doesn't eat any of them. It is the first time he's ever been able to eat so many sweets without getting into trouble. It's the first time he's ever had dessert for dinner and his parents were only encouraging it.

But while the rest of her family are relishing the calorie-free banquet, Nora doesn't care to eat any of it. As a picky eater, she doesn't really like eating any of this stuff. She doesn't really like any food at all. And since it has no nutrition, there's no real point to eating it. She just asks her grandma to make her a cheese quesadilla and eats some of that and a few bites of cherry pie. Then she's done. She watches her family eat and counts the minutes before it's time to go to bed.

"Too bad we can't have a good bottle of wine with this meal," Nora's father says.

Grandma says, "Well, you can, it just won't get you drunk."

The father shrugs and says, "Yeah, and what's the point of that?"

"I'm going to really miss wine when I die," Claire says with a drumstick of duck in her mouth. She turns to her husband. "Remind me to drink as much wine as possible whenever I get the chance from now on. I need to enjoy it while it lasts."

The grandma laughs at her daughter's comment, but Claire didn't seem to be joking whatsoever. Nora can tell that her mother's absolutely serious about getting all the drinking in that she can before she's stuck in a sober lifestyle for all eternity.

CHAPTER
THREE

An hour after dinner, Nora's parents put Jack to bed early because they're worried about him being a hyperactive pain in the butt after eating so many sweets. Although Jack can't get a sugar high in Heaven, he can still have a psychosomatic response to it and they decided it would be best to lie him down before it has a chance to kick in, just to be on the safe side.

Nora is alone with her grandmother, sitting on the couch with her. The young woman is basically a stranger to her, but she still has the voice and mannerisms of the grandma she knew a few weeks ago. She keeps asking Nora questions about her social life and how she's doing in school, but Nora doesn't really care to give her much of a response to any of it. Her grandmother can tell she's bored and depressed.

"What's wrong, little one? Don't you like getting to spend some time in Heaven?"

Nora shrugs, staring at the flames crackling in the fireplace.

"I just don't get it," Nora says.

"Don't get what?"

"Heaven. Why does it exist? What's the point of living on Earth your whole life and then dying and going to Heaven for all eternity?"

Her grandmother laughs. "Whoa, that's a deep question for a nine-year-old. Are you asking me to tell you the meaning of life?"

Nora shrugs. "I guess…"

Her grandmother inches closer to her on the couch. "Well, I learned the meaning of life the day I arrived in Heaven. Want to know what it is?"

Nora looks up at her. "You really know?"

Grandma nods. "Uh-huh. It's a big secret, though. Not even your mother and father know the meaning of life. Do you think you're mature enough to handle such knowledge?"

Nora's eyebrows perk up. "Yeah, I am. I'm the most mature 9-year-old in my whole school."

"Well, in that case, I guess you can handle it." She smirks and then looks around to make sure her daughter and her son-in-law don't hear. She leans in closer and explains in a hushed tone, "So it turns out that after people die, we become the batteries of the universe. Our souls generate energy that makes the sun shine bright and the stars twinkle and the Earth go from day to night. All stars and all planets need this energy. Without it, the universe would die."

Nora makes a confused face at her grandma. She's not sure if she's telling her the truth or just messing with her. It doesn't seem like it could possibly be the truth.

Her grandma continues, "We just have to live in Heaven and be happy in order to produce this energy. The happier we are, the more fuel we produce. This is why Heaven is such a paradise. It is a perfect place for us to generate happiness for all eternity, to be great producers of positive energy."

Nora isn't convinced. She says, "Then why does anyone go to Hell?"

"People in Hell produce energy, too," her grandma explains. "But it's negative energy. They live in eternal misery and suffering so that they can generate it. Both positive and negative energy are necessary for the universe to continue, so they are equally important. The purpose of your life on Earth is to determine which type of energy you'll be better at emitting once you die. You can either live a good, happy, positive lifestyle or you can be a source of negativity. It's up to you."

"I thought people went to Hell as punishment for being evil."

"It's not about punishment. There are plenty of good people who go to Hell and evil people who go to Heaven. For instance, people who are sad all the time always go to Hell. Depressed and traumatized people are great sources of negative energy. Some bad people go to Heaven, too, if they don't realize the horrible things they do are bad or if they have no guilt for their crimes. We call them sociopaths. But most people who go to Hell, like your grandfather, were bad because they were miserable. They hated themselves and so they did bad things. That's why there's the misconception that you go to Hell for being evil. It's just about what kind of energy you emit into the world."

When Nora hears this, she starts to get a little nervous. If her grandma is serious about this, it means that she's most likely destined to go to Hell. She's always been a very negative person and emits more negative energy than anyone she knows. She hopes her grandmother is just messing with her. She *prays* her grandmother is just messing with her. Because, otherwise, if she was to die tomorrow she would most certainly spend eternity in Hell producing negative energy for the universe.

Nora plays Pictionary with her family for a couple of hours, teamed up with her thirty-year-old grandma, and loses horribly because the dead woman can't draw for shit. Nora would have much rather played Settlers of Catan like they play at home, but because Grandma never heard of the game, she isn't able to make it materialize from her cupboard. Nora realizes that it must suck to die in a time when they didn't have a whole lot of fun things to do. Nora hopes she lives a long life just so that she'll have more interesting things to materialize in the afterlife. Games and books and even food will be far more varied and interesting when she's as old as her grandma was when she died. She plans to experience as much as she can in her life just so that her afterlife won't be as boring as her grandma's.

When it's time for bed, Nora is given her mom's childhood room, forced to sleep amongst three dozen porcelain dolls staring at her from the bookshelves. As Nora lies in bed, her covers up to her chin, she has to sleep with the light on, terrified that one of the dolls might come alive and attack her to steal her soul. Because she's in Heaven, she feels like anything is possible. Dolls can probably come alive here. And who knows what they'll do to a girl who called them stupid and boring when her mother tried to get her to play with them.

But after an hour of trying to sleep, none of the dolls come alive or attack. They just stare at her with their creepy glass eyes, holding their arms out like they're desperate to be hugged. She can't take it for much longer and covers up the doll collection with the sheet on her bed, blocking them from view.

Nora isn't very tired, so she tries to find something to occupy her time while the rest of the house is fast asleep. She goes through some old children's books from decades ago on her mother's bookshelf, but most of them are all blank. And those that aren't are only half-written. Nora assumes it's because her grandma never read any of these books, so she wasn't able to materialize anything but their covers from her memories.

Without any toys or books or games to play, Nora decides to draw some pictures. There are some colored pencils and construction paper in her mom's closet. Although she can't take the pictures home with her, she can give them to her grandma to keep in Heaven. Maybe they'll make her happy.

The only thing Nora can think of to draw is one of the tarantula flowers she saw on the drive over. She never got a good look at any of them, though. She wishes they would have stopped the car and picked one of the flowers so that she'd have one to draw now. She wonders if there's any in the vicinity of her grandma's house.

She knows it would be bad to leave the house in the middle of the night, but perhaps there's a flower bush close enough to see from the bedroom. She opens the curtains and looks out the window, peering across the dark purple landscape for the strangely shaped flowers.

Heaven doesn't get very dark at night, nor very light during the day. Because there's no sun in the afterlife and the concept of a night and day are mostly artificial, it never gets very bright or dark. It permanently feels like it's in a state of early dawn or late dusk.

The forest behind Grandma's house is just as lush and misty as it was on the road. There are red and white striped trees and black thorny bushes. But there's no sign of the tarantula flowers. Nora wonders if she shouldn't just draw one of the trees instead. They're a lot more interesting than the ones back home. She especially likes how the ground looks covered in the reddish-purple autumn leaves. It's like how she'd imagine Halloween would look in a fairy kingdom.

Nora decides to just draw the whole landscape. She's drawn landscapes before but they've always been from her head. It's exciting to draw one in person, especially one as interesting as this.

Nora pulls a little red chair from her mother's vanity

and sits in front of the window. Then she gets to work. Drawing the trees is easy enough. She draws trees at home all the time. They're one of her specialties. But the thing she has no idea how to draw is the mist and all the trees in the background that are fading into it. That's a technique of drawing that she's never been able to figure out.

As Nora examines the mist, wondering how she's going to render it onto the page, she sees something moving among the trees. At first, she thinks it's just the wind blowing through the branches but then she notices some figures in the mist. They are the same shadowy silhouettes she saw on the drive over, but these aren't standing still. They are moving, wandering through the woods. They are rather small, like children playing a game of hide and seek. Nora has no idea how or why they would be out there in the middle of the night.

"Must just be Heaven noise," she says to herself, even though she's still not sure what the heck Heaven noise actually is.

Her mother told her just to ignore the Heaven noise, but Nora doesn't want to. She thinks adding the shadowy figures to her drawing will make it a pretty cool picture.

As she shades in the background sky with black and purple colored pencils, she notices the shadowy figures coming closer. They step out of the mist and run through the backyard lawn of her grandmother's house. Nora only sees them for a second before they dash out of sight.

Curiosity gets the best of Nora. She wants to get a better look at the children, see what they're all about, figure out what they're doing in her grandma's backyard in the middle of the night. She puts down her drawing and sneaks out of her room, careful not to wake her parents sleeping on the other side of the wall.

A light shines beneath her grandma's door, brightening a section of the hallway. Because her grandma doesn't need sleep, she's surely still awake, probably knitting or reading or doing crossword puzzles like she always did when she was alive. Nora tiptoes past her door, not wanting her to realize she's sneaking around in the house when she should be asleep. She doesn't want to get yelled at for not doing what she was told.

In the living room, Nora steps carefully across the shag carpeting and around the dining room table to get to the window on the other side. She pulls open the curtain and sees the children in the yard. She's able to get a good look at them this time. They are all wearing the same horrible costumes that Nora's parents made her wear, with goat-like horns and reptile noses and pointy saber tooth tiger fangs hanging from their mouths. They look like angry little devils frolicking in the woods.

Nora can't tell what they're doing. They aren't playing hide-and-seek. They seem to be gathering mushrooms or acorns. Or maybe they're collecting pretty stones. Whatever they're doing, they seem to be scanning the area as though searching for hidden things, like they're on some kind of Easter egg hunt in Heaven.

But as she watches more carefully, she realizes that there's something seriously wrong with these children. They don't move or act like any kids she's ever seen. They're more like animals than civilized people. And then Nora realizes that the costumes they're wearing aren't costumes at all. The horns, the fangs, the patchy patterns and scraggly hair—it's all part of their bodies. They are the hideous creatures that the costumes were designed to resemble.

Nora recoils when she comes to this realization and her sudden movement catches their eyes. The strange children look in her direction, glaring at her with glowing orange eyes. As they move closer, her heart pounds in her chest, her hands shake, her eyes unable to look away as they come right up to the window and press their monstrous faces against the glass. They stick out their snake-like tongues and wiggle them side to side like they want to get a taste of her.

As they scratch at the glass, trying to get inside, Nora screams and tears the curtains shut, blocking them from her view.

"What's going on?" her grandma yells, charging into the living room and flipping on the light switch. "What are you doing out here?

Nora just backs away from the curtains and points at the window. When her grandmother understands what has frightened the girl, her eyes widen in shock.

"Oh my god, you weren't looking out the window

without your mask, were you?" she asks.

Nora can't speak. She can still hear them on the other side of the curtain, scratching on the glass, trying to get inside.

"Were you?" her grandma raises her voice. But she doesn't have to ask again to know the answer to the question.

She goes to the curtains and peeks outside. "Are they out there? Did they see you?"

The scratching stops the second her grandma peeks outside. She looks around, but Nora can tell she doesn't see anything. They've already run off.

Her grandma goes to her and kneels down. She holds Nora's shoulders tightly and looks her dead in the eyes.

"Nora, this is very, very important. Did the goblins see you? If they did, you're in great danger. You have to tell the truth."

Tears roll down Nora's cheeks. She's so scared and flustered that she doesn't know what to say. She just nods her head and hugs her grandma. She has no idea what she's just done but she knows it must have been very, very bad.

CHAPTER
FOUR

e◞

Nora's parents wake up to the commotion and race into the living room. They're pulling on their robes, racing to her daughter's cries like she must be hurt, like they need to rush her to the emergency room even though no such thing exists for living people in Heaven.

"The goblins saw her without her mask on," Grandma says to her daughter.

Claire panics when she hears this. "What did you just say?"

Grandma explains, "She was looking out the window."

Claire's expression goes from shock to anger. She races to her daughter and yells right in her face, "How could you be so stupid? I told you how important it is to wear your mask."

Nora cries louder. "I thought I only had to wear it outside."

"You have to wear it when looking out the windows, too. Don't you know how bad it is if a goblin sees you?"

Between sobs, Nora explains, "I didn't know they were goblins. You said they were just Heaven noise. I didn't think it was a big deal."

"Heaven noise?" her grandma asks. "What the heck is Heaven noise?"

The grandma looks over at her daughter, but Claire doesn't know what to say. It's obvious she just made it up because she didn't want to tell her daughter the truth.

When she finally explains, Claire says, "I just… I didn't want to scare her. She was going to have nightmares if she knew there were goblins in Heaven."

"If you just told me about the goblins, I would have been more careful," Nora says.

Claire sneers at Nora for talking back, holding up her hand like she wants to slap her.

But the grandma takes Nora's side. She asks her daughter in a severe tone, "Why would you lie to her about something so important? She's a smart girl. She could have handled it."

Claire is so frustrated that she turns away and screams. It's almost like she's more upset that it's her fault than she is that Nora's in danger. She goes to the other side of the room and paces around the coffee table, biting her nails and stewing in her vexation.

As Nora's grandma holds and comforts her, patting her head and trying to get her to relax, her father goes to Claire to figure out how to fix the situation.

He asks her in a calm voice, "What are we going to do? The goblins are going to come for her now."

He tries to speak quietly so that their daughter doesn't hear, but their voices aren't nearly hushed enough.

"I don't know," Claire says, not making eye contact with him.

"Do we take her back home? They can't get her if we go back to Earth. We should go right now."

Claire shakes her head. "That won't work. They won't let her leave. The gateway will reject her."

"Well, we've got to do something." He picks up the guidebook he got from the security guard at Heaven's gate. "Maybe there's instructions in here somewhere."

As he flips through the pages of the pamphlet, the grandmother kisses Nora on the cheek and then goes to her parents.

"There's only one thing to do about this," she says. Her voice is soft but imposing. She's never sounded more serious in their lives. "We have to offer her to the goblins and pray that they reject her."

Claire looks at her mother with disgust. "Are you crazy? That's the last thing we should do."

The grandma shakes her head. "It's the only way. If we try to run or protect her from them, they'll only want her even more. They enjoy hunting little girls like Nora and if she resists their blood thirst will never be quenched until they capture her. And when that happens, they'll never let her go."

Nora's parents go quiet. They don't seem to know what else to say. The grandmother is the expert in these matters. She's the only one who lives in Heaven and understands all of the rules. They have no choice but to listen to her.

Nora's grandmother looks over at the frightened

little girl with a sympathetic face and says, "I'm sorry, little one, but it's the only way."

Claire tells Nora to go into Jack's room and kiss him goodbye while he's sleeping. Nora doesn't want to, but her mother insists. She says that there's a chance she'll never be able to see him again. After saying goodbye to her little brother, her father pats Nora on the head and wishes her good luck. He's staying behind to watch over Jack while they're gone so this is his way of saying farewell. Even though they might never see each other again, he doesn't hug her goodbye. Her father always felt uncomfortable hugging people, even his own children, so this is the closest kind of affection Nora ever receives from her father.

Then Claire and her mom take Nora on the road. They drive her far away from the house, taking her to a place where the goblins play. Nobody will explain to her what's going on or why she has to go. They yell at her a lot and order her to take this seriously. They treat her like a bad girl who's always being a nuisance to all of them.

In the car ride there, Nora's mother is aggravated. She snaps at her daughter and her mom whenever anybody makes a sound. She's so upset that Nora is afraid to even breathe too heavily. But there are things Nora needs to know. The only reason she's in this mess is because her mother didn't tell her the truth. If her life is in danger she needs as much information as she can get in order to survive.

"Why do I have to go to the goblins?" Nora asks. "They're so ugly and scary."

Her mother answers in a harsh tone. "You're going to the goblins because you didn't listen to us. That's why."

It's exactly the explanation she'd expect from her mother. She decides it would be better to ask her grandmother instead.

"What are the goblins, Grandma?" she asks, blocking her mother completely from the conversation. "I thought Heaven was a happy place. Why do goblins live here?"

Claire lets out a long sigh, as though trying to cut the conversation short. But the grandmother doesn't pay any attention to her. She reaches into the backseat and takes her granddaughter's hand.

"The goblins were once children like you," she explains to Nora. "They are the souls of little boys and girls who died when they were very young."

Nora is startled by this revelation. "All children become goblins when they die?"

Her grandma laughs and shakes her head. "Not all of them. When children die, they never go to Hell. All children go to Heaven. But those who are unhappy, all the bad little kids who think only negative thoughts and are hateful toward the world, are transformed into goblins once they cross over. Even babies will become goblins if they are unhappy enough."

"Goblin babies?" Nora cries, completely startled by the idea.

But her grandma doesn't comment on Nora's reaction. She continues, "Since they don't produce happy energy, they have to serve a different purpose in the afterlife. It's their job to seek out and remove any negative influences in Heaven. They are drawn to negativity. It's like food for them. They pull weeds from gardens to keep them from getting ugly. They steal bad dreams from your heads while you sleep. They take all the bad memories away from us so that we can only focus on the good ones. They're an important part of the ecosystem in Heaven.

"But once they developed a gateway between the world of the living and the world of the dead, people from Earth started crossing over and bringing all their negativity with them. This made them targets of the goblins. The lost children try to weed them out of paradise. That's why you dress in those costumes when you come here. It's so the goblins think you're one of them. If they see another goblin with negative energy they don't think there's anything out of place because goblins are supposed to emit negative energy. They are made of nothing but bleakness and disgust."

Nora nods her head, thinking about what her grandmother is saying. It seems to make sense to her. Because there's so much negativity in Nora, it would definitely be plausible that she'd be a ripe target for the goblins.

"So they want to kill me and eat me because I'm a negative person?" Nora asks.

Her grandmother shakes her head. "No, not you. Because you're a child, they want to make you one of them. Goblins are always seeking out children to increase their numbers. This is because children who come to Heaven never start out as goblins. They get to live in paradise just like everyone else. But the children who don't think it's good enough, who criticize and complain about everything, who are never happy no matter how many wonders Heaven has to offer them—these are the children who are targeted by the goblins and taken away to join their numbers. That's what they want to do to you."

"So why are you taking me right to them?" Nora asks.

Her grandmother smiles at her and squeezes her fingers together. "Because you're going to show those nasty goblins that you're way too good for the likes of them."

Claire takes a small dirt trail off the main road and drives slowly into the woods. Red and purple leaves fall like snowflakes over the car as they travel toward their destination.

"There it is," the grandma says, pointing at a wooden structure up ahead.

They arrive at the thickest, tallest tree in the forest—a red wood behemoth that dwarfs everything else in the woods, like it's more mountain than timber. It has been converted into a massive treehouse twelve stories high. There are rope ladders and tire swings and bridges going between the colossal branches. Nora would have thought it was an impressive sight if it wasn't so old and creepy. The wood is blackened and dead. Rusty nails sticking out everywhere. If there has ever been a haunted treehouse before, this place would be it.

"This is the playhouse of the goblins," the grandmother says. "You have to wait for them in there."

"What do I do when they come?" Nora asks.

Her grandma gives Nora her costume. "Keep this on. It probably won't help since they already have your scent, but if you're lucky they'll just think you're one of them and let you go."

"What if she's not lucky?" Claire asks in an annoyed tone.

"Then you have to prove you're not like them," Grandma tells Nora. "You have to show them that you're a happy little girl full of enthusiasm and lust for life."

Claire yells, "How is she supposed to do that when she's scared out of her mind?"

Grandma looks Nora in her eyes. "I have faith in her. She's a good girl. And she's smart as a whip. She'll prove to them that she's not goblin material."

They open the car doors and pull Nora out into the misty woods. She puts on her costume quickly before any of the goblins see her. Then she looks back at her mother and grandmother with an expression of terror in her eyes.

"You're just going to leave me out here?" Nora asks

them. "Aren't you going to stay and help?"

The grandma shakes her head. "That will only complicate things. You have to stay here until morning. You have to wait until the goblins come to you, size you up and then leave you alone. If they have any interest in you then you'll never be safe. But once they reject you, they'll never bother you again, not for the rest of your life."

At the thought of being left alone, Nora goes into a panic. "But they're going to kill me! I don't want to be a goblin! I don't know how to think happy thoughts! They're going to turn me into one of them!"

"Just stop complaining and be happy, Nora!" her mom cries. "Put a smile on your face and stop being so miserable all the time!"

Nora glares at her mother and says, "I'm only miserable because of you."

Claire smirks. "Go on and think that. See what happens to you. The goblins probably love girls who think so poorly of their mothers."

Nora's grandmother gets between them. "You're only making it worse, Claire. Just have faith in your daughter."

Claire argues, "You're only on her side because all the negativity has been wiped from your mind. You used to be far more antagonistic than me. You're just as much a bitch as I am."

"Stop it with the pessimism," Grandma says. "You need to fill her with love and security. Don't you want her to be able to go back home with you?"

"Of course I do!" Claire cries. "What kind of mother do you think I am?"

This exchange continues for several minutes and only gets worse, but Nora is in too much shock to pay attention or get involved. She doesn't know why her mother is always like this. Whenever she needs her the most, her mother always gets so mad and annoyed. She just snaps at everyone around her. It's like she can't handle it when being a parent gets too difficult. It's like she thinks it's unfair that she has these responsibilities that she didn't know were going to be so challenging and so she takes it out on her children who just want her to be there for them.

Nora can't believe any of this is happening to her. She wishes at least her grandmother would give her some kind words of encouragement.

Before she knows what's happening, Nora's mom and grandma are hugging her and kissing her goodbye with all their strength. Then they get back into the car, telling her they'll pick her up midday tomorrow.

Before they drive off, her grandmother rolls down the window and says, "When all else fails, just laugh at the goblins. They won't know what to do with you if you just smile and laugh."

And then they're gone. They drive off down the dirt road, leaving her all alone in the haunted forest.

CHAPTER
FIVE

Nora stands there beneath the colossal tree, looking up at it like she's an insect staring up at a giant twisted beast. The thing looks skeletal and angry, with very little leaves and gnarled branches that reach out to the purple sky like scorpion tails. The treehouse seems like the kind of place where witches would live or maybe the children of witches. It seems to have been designed as a playhouse, but nobody has played here in a very long time. She has no idea how a place like this could belong in Heaven, the place that she thought was supposed to be an eternal paradise. If she ever visits Hell, this is what she would expect to find the first day she was there.

Looking around the trunk of the tree, she's not sure how to climb up into the treehouse. She doesn't really want to go up there at all, but it seems safer than staying out in the open. She can't believe her mother left her here without any help. They could have at least waited until she found her way up.

After circling the skyscraper-sized trunk, she finally

finds the closest thing that resembles a way up. There are a series of rotten boards going up the back of the tree toward the rickety structure above. Nora goes around one last time, but it seems this is the only way she'll be able to climb up.

"Are you kidding me?" she says to herself, looking up the makeshift ladder.

The boards look so weak and unstable, held together with rusty nails that will probably cut her up and give her tetanus. It's such a high climb that if one of the boards gives way she'll fall to her death. It won't matter if the goblins get her or not. She'll be dead before they even show up. And if she dies now, she'll end up turning into a goblin for sure.

She takes the ladder one board at a time, stepping carefully not to get hooked on a nail and gripping every rung with all the strength she has. It's even more difficult while wearing the stupid goblin costume. The mask makes it difficult for her to see. The clothing is bagging and gets caught on every twig she passes. But she forces herself up until she climbs up onto the first ledge of the treehouse and rolls over on her back to catch her breath.

"Why was that so damned hard?" Nora cries as she looks up at the branches and higher treehouse floors above her.

The wood is weak and bends under her weight as she gets herself to her feet. She's on some kind of balcony that circles the trunk. There's a railing on the edge but it seems so weak that she'd rather use the actual tree for support instead. The last thing she needs is for the railing to give way and have her break her neck on the way down.

The forest is even more haunting and beautiful from up here. She takes a moment to stare out across the landscape, wishing she could take a picture or make a drawing. After breathing it in for a moment, trying to think of happy thoughts, she moves on. She cautiously walks around the trunk of the tree to a set of stairs that lead up to the next level. She has no idea what she'll find up there, but she knows she needs to find a better area to spend the rest of the night. It needs to be a bigger, wider section of the tree fort. She doesn't want to deal with worrying about loose boards and rusty nails when she knows there are goblins on the way.

She climbs up, level after level, until she finds the largest building in the treehouse. It's as big as some homes she's seen before, with windows and a front door and a shingled roof. If it wasn't such a rundown scary place, she could see herself living here. Every kid always dreams of living in a treehouse. If this place was fixed up it would be the ultimate treehouse anyone's ever seen, even better than the one from Swiss Family Robinson.

When Nora tries to open the door, something blocks it from the other side. It's either so old that it's rotted into place or somehow it's been barred or locked shut. Nora pushes all her weight against the door, huffing and puffing to force it open, but she just can't seem to make it budge.

Then a voice comes from the other side. "What's the password?"

When Nora hears this, she stumbles backward, nearly tumbling over the edge of the railing to her death. It sounded like a normal boy but how the heck would there be a boy hanging out in this old, abandoned treehouse? She wonders if he's a ghost. He sounded perfectly real and normal, but why else would there be someone up here? Although there doesn't seem to be any logical reason for there to be a ghost in Heaven, Nora is sure that's the only explanation.

A boy pops his head out the window, wearing a bright orange goblin mask. When they meet each other's gaze, he holds up his fist in the air.

"I said what's the password?" he repeats. "Do you want me to force you to walk the plank?"

It's definitely not a ghost. It's just another kid like Nora. Maybe a year or two younger, but he's definitely real. He's just kind of weird.

"Stop fucking with her and let her in," another voice says. It's a girl's voice. Someone older than both Nora and the boy. She peeks out the window and waves. "Hi, there. We thought you might be a goblin. You're not a goblin, are you?"

Nora gives her a dirty look. "No! Do I look like a goblin?"

"Kind of," the girl says.

Nora looks down at her outfit and sees what she means, even though both of them are wearing goblin costumes as well. She's surprised to see the two children but kind of relieved she's not alone. She never thought she'd ever find other kids up in the treehouse.

When the weird kids open the front door of the treehouse, the girl asks, "Did the goblins see you, too?"

Nora nods.

"Same with us," she says, unlocking the door and holding it open so Nora can enter. "Guess we're all in the same boat."

Nora is shocked there are others who have been seen by goblins at the same time as her. She assumed she would be all alone. She was sure she would have to face this all by herself. Knowing that there are others like her puts her mind at ease. It makes her feel like she might actually pull through if she has others to help.

She asks, "How long have you been here?"

The older boy comes to the door and says, "Hours, days, who knows?"

When Nora enters, she can't believe how large and elaborate the treehouse looks on the inside. It's still rickety and rundown, but it looks like a real house, with a dining room table and chairs, an old-fashioned kitchen with a sink that gets water from a wooden barrel, a counter with shelves and cabinets. Even something that resembles a refrigerator but is made of wood and probably couldn't preserve any food at all without at least a block of ice in there like they used in the olden days.

The place is drafty and dark. The only light comes from fat, half-melted candles made of earwax that emit a foul odor. Old rags cover the windows like curtains but don't keep out any of the frosty wind. Every inch of the floor is rotten and splintered. It would be seriously dangerous if she walked on it barefoot.

Once Nora's fully inside, the other two kids close the door and lock it tightly with a rusted latch. They seem excited to see her, like they haven't seen anyone in the treehouse for a very long time.

"I'm Mason," the boy says, leaning toward Nora like he already has a crush on her.

He's wearing a costume different from hers. It's covered in orange hair with a big wide-nostril nose. He looks a bit like Animal from the Muppets but with sad eyes and wrinkled human lips.

Nora introduces herself and shakes his cold, pasty hand.

"That's Trish," he says, pointing at the tall girl with sunburnt skin and angry eyes.

Nora shakes Trish's hand even though she doesn't seem to want to. The girl wears a bright purple costume with black feathers hanging from the sides. She doesn't seem very happy, like she spends most of her time lying in bed feeling sorry for herself.

"So welcome to our treehouse," Mason says. "It's pretty cool, isn't it? It's ours but you're welcome to stay if you want."

"I thought this place belonged to the goblins," Nora says.

Mason shakes his head. "No way. If the goblins come here, I'll beat their asses." He runs across the rickety floor to the dining room and retrieves a wooden club that appears to have once been the leg of a table. "I'm the great defender of this fort and goblins aren't allowed."

Nora isn't sure if he's serious or just putting on an act. "You're going to fight the goblins?"

He swings his table leg in the air as though pretending he's in a swordfight. "Yeah. If a goblin comes, I'll knock his head off."

"But there's going to be dozens of them," she says. "You can't fight off that many."

"I don't care how many there are. I'll kill any one of them who tries to get me."

"*Can* you kill them?" Nora asks. "Aren't they already dead?"

Mason shrugs. "So what if they're already dead. I'll just kill them again."

Nora doesn't know what to make of the hyperactive boy with the table leg. He seems pretty confident that he's going to defeat the goblins for some reason. Nora thinks he might be a little crazy.

"Just ignore him," Trish says, sitting at the table and playing solitaire with a deck of faded moldy cards. "He's been acting brave like that forever, but he's really scared shitless. He knows he doesn't stand a chance."

Mason lowers his club and turns to her, "Shut up, I'm not scared!"

Trish shrugs. "Could have fooled me." Then she

goes back to playing cards.

Nora says, "You shouldn't try to fight them. My grandmother said we have to be happy and put on a positive face. If we laugh and smile like we're having fun, then they won't want us."

Trish laughs out loud and shakes her head. "You actually believe that?"

Nora turns to her. "Yeah, my grandma told me it was how to stop the goblins from taking me away."

"Your grandma's a liar just like everyone else in this place," Trish says.

Nora goes to the table and sits down across from her as Mason continues swinging his club in the background.

"What do you mean?" Nora asks.

Trish keeps her eyes on her cards, barely interested in the conversation. She says, "They bring children here to turn them into goblins. Once you arrived your fate was sealed. There's no way out of it."

"But why would my grandma lie? She's the only one in my family who never lies to me."

"Your grandma will get perks for bringing you here. Her domain will grow. Her light will burn brighter. She'll get more traveling privileges. It doesn't matter if you're her granddaughter. People will sell out their own family members to get a better piece of eternal bliss."

Nora can't believe that could possibly be true. Her grandmother was never the greedy type. "Why would she get perks just for turning me into a goblin?"

"Because Heaven needs goblins, just like a garden needs worms. But there's never enough. People need encouragement to turn over their children or else they might hide them forever."

Trish's words seem so bleak and pessimistic. She can't possibly be telling the truth. But it was kind of strange how her grandmother rushed her to this place in the middle of the night and left her all by herself. If Nora had a loved one that she didn't want to be turned into a goblin she would stay with them all night long and keep them happy and cheered up. She would do whatever it takes to stop the goblins from getting them. Her grandma was very nice and supportive, but she didn't seem like she really did everything she possibly could to help out. It's like her whole goal was just to get her here and that's it. She wonders if Trish might be right.

"Then what are we going to do?" Nora asks.

Trish shrugs and keeps playing her card game. Nora can't believe she's taking all this so calmly. She doesn't seem to care about what happens to her, like she stopped worrying about living a long time ago.

"There's got to be a way out of this?" Nora continues. "We can't just wait for the goblins to take us."

Trish doesn't seem to want anything to do with Nora anymore. "You can try to fight them with the dumbass over there if you want, but you'd just be wasting your time. Better to just give up and enjoy the little time you have left as a human."

"This is such bullshit." Nora gets out of her seat and

paces around the room, the rickety boards squeaking and bending beneath her feet. "I didn't even want to come to this stupid place. I wanted to stay home and play by myself, but my dumb parents forced me to visit my grandma in Heaven and now I'm going to turn into a goblin. If I could've done what I wanted none of this would have happened." She kicks a rusty bucket across the floor. "It's so unfair!"

After she says this, Trish drops the cards in her hand. Mason lowers his table leg. They both look at her. Their eyes are wide with astonishment.

"Wait a minute..." Trish says. "Are you saying you're still alive?"

Nora looks at her, not sure what she's asking.

"You're just on a trip with your family?" Mason asks, approaching her with concerned eyes.

Nora nods. "Yeah, aren't both of you?"

They just stare at her and shake their heads.

"Both of us are dead," Mason says.

Trish stands up and says, "I died in a car accident because my asshole father was driving drunk. He survived but I went through the windshield because of a faulty seatbelt in his shitty old pickup truck."

Mason says, "I got bit by a rattlesnake when I was playing war in the desert behind my house. It got me in the neck while I was hiding in the bushes. No one found me in time."

Nora backs away from them, almost afraid, like she's hanging out with a couple of ghosts.

She says, "But why are you wearing those costumes?

I thought only visitors dressed like goblins."

Trish is confused by her question.

"We're not wearing costumes," she says, gripping the feathers growing out of the side of her head. "This is part of us now."

Nora can't believe what she's saying. It looks like they're wearing masks. She can still see their human eyes and human mouths. They still have a lot of normal skin showing. They don't look like goblins at all. But when she examines more carefully, she can tell that their masks are fused to their skin. The horns and fangs and distorted features are a part of them. They really are turning into goblins.

"How long have you been here exactly?" Nora asks.

"Hours, days, who knows?" Mason says, repeating what he said earlier.

Trish laughs. "More like weeks or months. Our families ditched us here, saying we had too much negative energy and didn't deserve a place in Heaven. We've been turning into goblins ever since."

Nora can't believe she's been hanging out with goblins this whole time. She's not sure what she should do. She wonders if they've both been testing her this whole time, trying to make her see things in a negative light so that she would join them and become goblins like them. She wonders if she shouldn't run away.

"I'm not a goblin!" Mason yells.

Trish grabs one of the horns sticking out of his head. "What's this then, idiot? You're more goblin than I am."

Mason pulls himself out of her grip and cries, "I'm

not a goblin yet! I'll never become a full goblin!"

Trish laughs. "You're just kidding yourself. All of us will be goblins sooner or later. Just you wait."

"Screw that!" Mason yells and slams his table leg three times into the coffee table until splinters fly into the air.

Nora doesn't know what else to do. She just breaks into tears and covers the eye holes of her mask. "But I don't want to turn into a goblin…"

Trish gets in her face. "Well, too bad. You're stuck here just like the rest of us. You're going to be a goblin whether you like it or not."

Nora shakes her head. "Grandma said I could get out of this."

"Your grandma's a liar and a bitch," Trish says. "Only the worst kind of person would bring her granddaughter here before she's even dead. Your grandma doesn't love you at all."

Nora runs toward the door of the treehouse. She tries to pull open the latch but it won't budge, like it's rusted shut.

"Where do you think you're going?" Trish asks.

"I'm getting out of here!" Nora cries. "I'm going back to my grandma's house and telling my parents on her."

Trish laughs. "This is the goblin's playhouse. Do you really think they'll let you leave here?"

Nora tugs on the door but she still can't get it open. Trish goes to her and grabs her by the neck. She pulls her to a window and points out into the woods.

"See that?" Trish asks, pointing to the distance.

There are several figures in the forest coming out of the mist, surrounding the treehouse. "They're already here. They're already coming for you."

Nora wiggles out of her grip and backs away.

"Because you're still alive, they're going to be more interested in you than either of us," Trish says. "They want to make sure to make you one of them before you have a chance to escape back to the world of the living. They're going to come for you tonight."

Nora shakes her head. "I won't let them get me."

Trish smiles. "You're going to be a goblin by morning. Just you wait."

Although the goblins surround the tree below, they don't climb up to get them. At least not yet. They're just wandering around down there, stalking through the forest, as though they're more interested in keeping Nora from escaping than they are trying to come for her.

Nora's not sure what to do. She can't try to leave but doesn't want to give up like Trish. She has to think of another way out of her situation. There's a chance that her grandma wasn't lying to her, that all she has to do is think positive thoughts and try to be happy and avoid wallowing in the helplessness of the situation. But she's not sure how to do that. Having other kids with her who don't seem to have any positive energy in them whatsoever is making it difficult for her. At first, she thought it would be better to have others going through the same situation as her. But now she thinks it might have been better to have done it on her own.

"Is there anything to eat?" Nora asks the other kids. "I'm hungry."

Mason frowns. "Yeah, but it's just goblin food."

"Goblin food?" Nora asks.

Mason goes to the wooden refrigerator and pulls out a bowl of bubbling gruel. He brings it to the dining room table and drops it down in front of her. "Goblin food."

Nora stares down into the clay bowl and recoils at the smell. Even though it's bubbling, it's not hot or even warm. It bubbles for some other reason. Mason gives her a wooden spoon and Nora gives it a try. The taste is bitter. It's like mud and oatmeal and bacon grease mixed together in a room-temperature porridge.

"That's nasty," Nora says, pushing the bowl away.

Both Mason and Trish laugh at her for actually eating some of it. But after a few minutes, hunger gets the better of her and she takes five more bites. She eats them quickly, swallowing them before they even touch her tongue. It's just an illusion, so she knows it won't make her sick. She just needs something to take the hunger away.

"So you can make stuff materialize like my grandmother can?" Nora asks them.

At first, they don't know what she means by that.

But then they think about it a little and realize that she is talking about how they pulled a bowl of food out of the refrigerator like magic. It's the same as how Nora's grandmother pulled all the delicious food from her oven when they had a feast earlier that day.

Mason says, "Yeah, we can create stuff like we did back in our dwellings, but it's not the same as before. Everything we create in the treehouse sucks. It's all goblin stuff. None of it is any good."

Mason goes to a wooden toy box on the other side of the room and opens the lid. He pulls out a checkerboard.

"See?" Mason says. "I was trying to pull out a video game system, but I only got checkers."

Nora gets a good look at the checkerboard. Not only is the board made of rotten wood, but half the checkers are missing. There's no way anyone could have fun with such a piece of junk. She looks over at Trish's cards on the dining table and realizes she probably got them from the box as well. It's like this place is designed to be disappointing to children so that they stay bored and disappointed and trapped in a negative state of mind.

"What else can you get?" Nora asks, just curious to see if any of it is of any use.

Mason pulls more stuff out of the box. He hands her a broken plastic helicopter, a yoyo without a string, a single Lego, a Tonka truck without wheels, a rusted knotted up slinky, a headless Barbie doll, a rubber band ball that smells like burnt hair. It's all just a bunch of disappointment.

"See," Mason says. "Just goblin stuff."

Nora sits down on the splintered wood floor and stares at all the items spread out before her. She wonders if there's something she can do with them. As somebody who has always been perpetually bored, she's always found ways to amuse herself even with stuff that she thought was useless junk. To her, a Barbie mansion isn't any different from a yoyo without a string. The fanciest, most popular toy in the world might as well be just a piece of junk from a goblin's toy box. But she always finds a way to make it interesting.

"Hmmm…" Nora says, holding up the headless Barbie and the rusted slinky. "Have you two been bored out of your minds up here this whole time?"

They both nod.

"Is it because you had nothing fun to play with?" she asks.

They shrug.

"Maybe you just lack imagination, then," Nora explains. "Because all this stuff could keep me interested for days. I've always found broken toys to be way more fun than normal ones."

She wraps the headless Barbie up in the rusted slinky until it looks like some kind of monstrous metal snake woman. When the other kids see it, they think it looks weird and cool. Even Trish kind of likes it.

"I can teach you how to turn this place into a paradise better than anywhere else in Heaven," Nora says. "We can show the goblins we're not sad, bored, negative kids who don't know how to be happy."

Although Trish is skeptical, Mason's eyes light up with hope. It's like they finally have a chance now that they have someone who can put a positive spin on their predicament. Maybe they'll just be able to make it out of the treehouse after all.

CHAPTER
SIX

Nora has Mason and Trish pull out dozens of toys from the toy box and scatter them across the room. It soon turns into some kind of museum of old broken relics. It's like a toy graveyard. It makes Nora wonder if all lost unloved toys on Earth eventually end up in the hands of disappointed goblins like them. The mass of ugly playthings only annoys Trish and confuses Mason, but Nora is sure there's a way she can use all of this stuff to her advantage.

"What exactly are you going to do with all this crap?" Trish asks, sitting far away from the toy mountain, as though just touching any of it would make her sick.

"We just have to have fun and the goblins will let us go, right?" Nora asks. "We're going to play with this stuff and show them we can be a source of happy energy."

Trish shakes her head. "It won't work. I already told you that it doesn't matter. The second you arrived here you were doomed to become a goblin."

"Have you even tried to resist it?" Nora asks. "Have

you tried to have fun for even a second since you got here?"

Trish looks at her for a moment and then shrugs. "Everything here's boring. Why bother?"

Nora explains, "This place is a test to see which kids are goblin-material and which aren't. It's supposed to make you want to give up and accept your fate. But if we try to make the most of what we have here, we might prove we're more than just goblins."

Trish doesn't seem convinced, but Mason is looking a little more hopeful.

"Do you think it will really work?" Mason asks.

Nora shrugs. "It's got to be better than doing nothing."

Nora and Mason get to work on creating new toys out of all the broken junk. At first, it seems too difficult even for Nora to come up with anything worthwhile to play with. So many faceless dolls and sticky limbless action figures. There's not much they can do with them. They try to have a battle between the broken soldiers and the broken dolls, imagining the dolls are giant mutant babies attacking a city. But it's difficult for Mason to get interested. He just smashes the soldiers against the dolls for a few seconds before he gets bored and tosses them away. Nora also isn't able to find any enjoyment in the game. She'd only enjoy it if she was able to witness real giant babies attacking real human soldiers. That would be a cool sight to see.

They try making artistic sculptures out of all the junk. They build human-shaped monstrosities as tall as them out of broomsticks, rocking horses, garbage-soaked stuffed animals, and broken glass bottles. Mason doesn't have a lot of fun with it because he doesn't have any artistic ability whatsoever, but Nora is quite happy with the final products. The room is now occupied by four new friends they can play with. Though the figures can't move, they can hold table-leg weapons and wear cardboard box helmets. They can help them keep guard over the treehouse.

Trish doesn't help out with anything. She just sits at the table, watching them with irritation in her eyes. She thinks what they're doing is stupid. Their games are stupid, their ideas are stupid, and thinking they can actually escape their fate is the stupidest thing of all.

"I know, let's play pirates," Nora says. "I'll be the captain and you'll be my first mate and these guys are our crew."

"Yeah! Pirates!" Mason cries. It's the first time he's shown enthusiasm for an idea Nora's come up with. "I'm the king of the pirates!"

"Okay, you can be the king of the pirates but I'm still your captain," Nora says.

"King of the pirates!"

They dig through the junk looking for stuff they can wear to look more like brigands of the sea. They make pirate hats and eye patches out of cardboard and rubber bands. Mason uses a curtain rag as a cape and

Nora ties half a broomstick to her left calf to resemble a peg leg.

"Who's Trish going to be?" Mason asks.

Nora shrugs. "Whoever she wants to be."

Trish responds, "I'm a ghost haunting your stupid ship. That means you can't see or touch or talk to me."

"No, Trish should be our prisoner!" Mason says. "Let's make her walk the plank!"

Nora thinks about it for a minute. "That's not a bad idea. We should make a plank for prisoners."

Trish doesn't even look up at them when she says, "You even think about touching me I'll throw both of you out of this treehouse and feed you to the goblins."

Nora just ignores the stubborn girl and asks Mason, "Materialize some wood for us. Every pirate ship needs a plank."

"On it!" Mason says, going to the closet to pull out boards of rotten wood.

"We also need grog," Nora says. "Every pirate drinks grog."

"What's grog?" Mason asks, carrying boards to the middle of the room, stepping carefully to avoid all the broken toys and miscellaneous junk.

Nora shrugs. "Just get some juice or Kool-Aid or something."

As Mason goes to the refrigerator, Nora digs out a bent bicycle wheel with a flat tire and says that it can be how they control the ship. She attaches it to an open window with a frayed jump rope and moves a chair in front of it. Then she sits down and pretends to sail the ship, even though it looks more like she's pretending to drive a car.

When Mason gets back with two smoking goblets of grog, he hands one to Nora and says, "It's gross. Just pretend to drink it."

But out of curiosity, Nora tries it anyway. Just takes a sip and then spits it out.

"What the heck!" Nora cries. "It tastes like gasoline!"

She continues spitting and rubbing her tongue on her costume.

"I think it *is* gasoline," Mason says.

Nora just coughs and gags as Trish laughs her ass off in the background.

For the next hour, Nora and Mason play pirates. They pretend the treehouse is their ship, the leaves and branches of the tree are the sail, and the goblins scurrying on the ground below them are vicious sea monsters trying to get them. But it's just not very entertaining for either of them. Maybe it's because Trish keeps criticizing them and making fun of them for playing a stupid game of make-believe like a couple of babies, or maybe it's because Nora is too worried about the goblins below to concentrate on having fun. Nora doesn't want to give up, but she doesn't know what else she should do. She's always been easily bored and finds it difficult to figure out how to fill her free time. Playing pirates isn't the kind of thing she would choose to do at home, so it's probably the wrong approach to take to make herself happy. All the ideas she's been coming up with are things she assumed Mason would be interested in. But she needs to come up with something to do that interests herself. Mason's already half-goblin. He probably doesn't have any hope left. Nora needs to focus on her own entertainment. She needs to do the kinds of things that she would normally find fun to do at home.

But she can't think of anything. Even the stuff she always did at home doesn't appeal to her at the moment. There's not much that makes her happy. She stops playing pirates with Mason and leaves the treehouse. She takes off her pirate accessories and goes to the rickety railing outside, staring down at the goblins below. Mason follows after her, wondering why she stopped playing.

"I don't know, maybe Trish is right," Nora says.

"What... We were having fun, weren't we?" Mason says. "I haven't had as much fun since I got here."

"So you want to keep playing?" Nora asks.

Mason thinks about it for a moment and then shrugs. "Maybe not..."

Nora can tell he was starting to get just as bored as she was. Playing pirates was just a waste of time. They need to do something more interesting than just playing with toys or pretending to be pirates. Nora is getting too old to find any of that stuff worthwhile. She doesn't think there's anything that can make her happy. She wonders if she's just not a happy kind of person. She wonders if maybe she should just embrace the idea of becoming a goblin.

"I guess I'll probably be spending the night," Nora says. "Do you have a place I can sleep?"

Mason nods. "We have a bedroom higher up in the tree. It has a lot of beds, but they're not comfortable and smell bad. We rarely ever go up there since we don't need to sleep."

Nora understands. She doesn't know if she'll be able to sleep in a goblin bed but she's getting tired and doesn't know what else to do.

"But if you sleep up there you have to watch out for Trish," Mason says, leaning in close so that the girl inside the treehouse doesn't hear. "She might try to eat you."

Nora is shocked by his words.

"Eat me?" she cries, almost loud enough for Trish to hear.

Mason nods. "She's tried to eat me before. Because the only food we can make here is gross goblin food, she cut off my leg when I was lying in bed and cooked it and ate it, hoping it would taste better than what we normally have."

Nora can't believe what he's saying. At first, she thinks he must be messing with her. But the look on his face proves that he's serious.

Mason continues, "She said I tasted gross because I'm half-goblin. But because you're human and still alive she'll probably think you'll taste better. You should watch out for her. She's not a very nice person."

The kid still has his leg so Nora assumes you can grow back limbs if you lose them in Heaven, but she's confused about why Trish would do such a thing. It's not like they need to eat to survive. She wonders if Trish was just bored or if she had phantom hunger pangs. Either way, she'll have to keep a close eye on the older girl. Because she's still alive, Nora has more to lose than either of these half-goblin children. She has enough to worry about without having to deal with the possibility of being cannibalized.

Nora follows the half-goblin boy higher up into the treehouse, climbing up wobbly staircases and across rope bridges that barely hold their weight. The treehouse stretches farther up the tree than she imagined it would, spreading out across the thick branches. There are dozens of smaller structures that are even more rickety and poorly put together than the main living quarters where they left Trish. The structures are small one-door, one-window rooms just big enough for a small bed and a nightstand. There are so many of them that they could accommodate at least fifty other children even if they each got their own little treehouse to themselves.

As Nora stares up into the little structures built higher up in the tree, she asks, "What are all those other buildings for?"

Mason looks at them for a second and then diverts his eyes. He shakes his head. "I don't know. I've never gone up that high before. It's too scary."

"You're scared of falling?" Nora asks. "But you're already dead. You wouldn't die if you fell even from this height."

"I don't care. It would still hurt. Trish pushed me out of the treehouse once as a joke and it was horrible. I never want that to happen ever again."

Nora understands what he means. She couldn't imagine falling from that height, even if she'd survive the fall. Even if it didn't hurt, it would still be so traumatic that she'd be scared of ever going high in a treehouse ever again.

"But I'm not just scared of falling," Mason continues. "I also wouldn't want to run into the grim lurker."

"Who's the grim lurker?"

"Trish says he's an old man who lives in the highest room at the top of the treehouse. He's a half-goblin like us but he's been there for years."

"An old man? I thought only children could be goblins."

"He's a hobgoblin."

"A hobgoblin?"

"They are adults with the minds of children."

"Like someone who's mentally handicapped?"

Mason nods. "They are treated the same as children when they die. But they don't go to Hell like other adults, even if they are negative and sad. They become hobgoblins."

Nora looks up into the trees. Some of the structures above are lit by candles, but she doesn't see any sign of anyone living up there. It's possible someone could be inhabiting the lofty structures, but it's also possible that Trish was just fucking with the young boy and trying to scare him, especially with such an obviously scary name like the grim lurker. He sounds like just a made-up boogie man.

"How do you know he's real?" Nora asks.

"Trish told me."

"Has she ever seen him?"

Mason shakes his head. "The kids who were here before Trish told her about him before they joined the goblins. And the kids before them said the same thing."

"So it's possible it's just a made-up ghost story?" Nora asks.

"Maybe…"

Just in case he is real, Nora has no interest in going up that high. She doesn't want to risk running into a half-hobgoblin man who has probably gone insane with loneliness.

"This way," Mason says, moving on.

He takes them to a room three stories up the trunk to the sleeping quarters. They have to take a rope ladder through a hatch in the floor to get inside. Two earwax candles are burning on crooked shelves on the wall. Five little beds made of boards and rusty nails with uneven legs and mold-caked headboards are crammed together so tightly in the small room that they might as well be a single five-person cot. The mattresses and pillows are stuffed with rat nests and torn in multiple places, the blankets are filthy leathery rags, and the whole room reeks of wet animal. Nora has no idea how she's going to sleep in such horrific accommodations.

"This is it?" Nora asks. "The beds are so gross."

"Yeah, they're goblin beds. It's the only way goblins sleep."

Nora climbs into the cleanest-looking bed and lies down. The second she hits the mattress a cloud of dust billows out accompanied by a foul odor, causing her to cough and gag. It's lumpy and uncomfortable. If she wasn't so tired, she'd never be able to sleep in it. But despite how disgusting it is, she already finds her eyes rolling shut.

"I'll leave you alone then," Mason says. "Sorry the beds are so gross. I hope you have a good sleep anyway."

Nora keeps her eyes closed as she says, "I'll be fine. I always have good dreams when I sleep."

That's Nora's new plan. The only plan she has left. She might not be able to figure out a way to be happy in the treehouse, but she knows how to be happy when she sleeps. Sleeping is one of her favorite things to do. At home, she makes sure to sleep as much as she can. She loves escaping from reality into a fantasy world where anything can happen. She's good at lucid dreaming and enjoys when her dreams are completely realistic yet she has total control over everything that happens. It's the thing that makes her happier than anything in the world. She wishes she could do it all the time.

But before Mason leaves, he says, "You won't have

any good dreams here. Only goblin dreams. You won't like them. It's why I never sleep here anymore."

Nora doesn't want to believe him. She waits until he leaves and lets herself fall asleep. She knows how to make good dreams. It doesn't matter where she is. She'll show the goblins they can't break her spirit if she can just get a good night's sleep. Even if her mattress was made of nails, even if her bed was full of bugs and spiders, if she can fall asleep she will definitely have the happiest of dreams.

CHAPTER
SEVEN

Nora's dreams are miserable. They are nothing like the dreams she has at home. Even when they are as realistic and vivid as they are when she has lucid dreams, she can't control anything. Everything turns out bad. They aren't nightmares, though. They are just sad and boring. She's in a field petting a cat with no eyes and sticky fur. Then she dreams about being covered in a blanket of frogs in a puddle of mud in the middle of the night. Then she dreams she's at home alone, but she doesn't have any games or toys to play with. Her family has moved out and taken everything with them, all the furniture and everything. It's just a big empty house with boring white walls and no television or food or electricity. She can't leave the house because the doors are locked and chained. The windows are boarded up. It's like she's a ghost haunting her old house with nothing to do.

When she wakes up, it feels as though she's only slept an hour or two. She doesn't feel well-rested or relaxed. She feels even worse than she did before she went to sleep. Her dreams were goblin dreams. They didn't make her happy or give her hope. They didn't allow her to escape from reality.

She sits up and notices Trish on the bed next to her, leaning against a headboard, holding a rusty butcher knife, and staring out the window in such a causal manner that it freaks Nora out. The second she sees her, Nora gets upright and grips the frame of the bed as though she wants to break off a board and use it as a club. Mason told her that she should watch out for Trish. He said that she might try to eat her like she tried to eat him. Seeing that butcher knife in the older girl's hand, Nora's sure that's what she's planning right now.

"What are you doing in here?" Nora asks.

Trish looks over at her and says, "Just sitting here. What's it to you?"

Nora looks at the knife and back up at the girl. Trish notices her discomfort and laughs.

"What you think I'm going to murder you or something?" Trish asks.

Nora can't help but be tense with her holding the knife, even though the girl has such a relaxed posture.

"You're not going to eat me, are you?" Nora asks.

Trish laughs even harder. "Eat you? Why the hell would I eat you?"

"Mason said you tried to eat him because the food here is terrible," Nora says.

Trish shakes her head. "And you actually believed him? Why would I do that? Even goblin food would taste better than human flesh."

"He didn't have any reason to lie."

Trish points the knife at her like she's pointing a finger. "Look, you don't know that kid like I do. He's a pathological liar. He's always saying things like that to get attention."

Nora doesn't know if she believes the girl as she continues, "He always pretends to be a victim so that people will feel sorry for him. When I first met him, he claimed that he died because he had abusive parents who beat him to death with a shovel for not picking up dog poop in the backyard. But then a few days later he forgot he told me that and said he died in a plane crash. He makes shit up like that all the time. Why do you think he's here? He's a pathetic miserable idiot who hates himself. Just like the rest of us."

"Then why are you carrying that butcher knife?" Nora asks.

Trish looks at it as though she forgot it was in her hand. "For protection. The goblins are getting restless. They've been climbing higher up in the tree than I've ever seen them." Trish looks her in the eyes. "Honestly, I'm getting a little scared."

Trish wasn't lying. The goblins are going crazy. They are climbing up the tree, dangling from branches, swinging in the tire swings, filling the landscape with their sadness and ugliness. The sight is horrifying to Nora, even though there's nothing particularly frightening about them. They look disgusting and move in cringe-inducing ways, but they don't seem particularly menacing. They are just miserable lost souls that exist only to absorb negative energy and make other sad children exactly like them.

"That's going to be you soon," Trish says, stepping up behind her. "They're coming for you."

Nora shakes her head. "I'm not going to let them."

Trish laughs. "You keep saying that, but the goblins keep coming closer. They would only do that if they knew you were losing hope."

"I've decided. I'm going to fight them."

"Good luck with that."

She points at the butcher knife in Trish's hands. "Can you make me more of those?"

"Sure, but it's not going to do you any good. The last kids I was with tried to fight the goblins. One of them was human like you. He fought them with knives and sticks and shovels, but that only made them come for him faster."

"I'm still going to try."

"Why bother? You can't possibly defeat that many of them, especially since they're already dead."

"But they can still feel pain, can't they?" Nora asks.

Trish pauses and thinks about it for a minute. "Everyone in Heaven feels pain as far as I know. I'm sure goblins are no different."

Nora points at the goblins in the tree like she's aiming a gun at them. "Then I'll hurt them so bad that they'll regret coming for me. I'll make them run away screaming."

Trish smiles. It's the first smile Nora's seen on her face that wasn't condescending. The older girl seems to be genuinely delighted by Nora's conviction.

"I'm going to make them feel so much pain that they'll have no choice but to let me go. By the end of the night, they're going to be terrified of me."

"What if it doesn't work? Just because you scare them off, you might still turn into a goblin."

"It doesn't matter. I'll still show them not to mess with me. If I'm going to be one of them, then I'll be the queen of the goblins."

Trish's eyes light up. She doesn't just look excited and optimistic by one of Nora's proposals, she seems absolutely thrilled by it.

"Hell yeah!" Trish yells. "Let's both become queens of the goblins!" Then she raises her butcher knife and shouts at the creatures below. "You hear that? We're going to fuck you up!"

With Trish on board, Nora's feeling more confident than ever. They go back to Mason in the main area of the treehouse and tell him the plan and he's immediately in favor of fighting the goblins. He raises his table leg and shouts with excitement.

"Let's beat up all those stupid goblins until they cry!" he says.

Then they get to work. They materialize dozens of

butcher knives and use broken jump ropes to tie them to the ends of broken broomsticks to create spears. They make a pile of large rocks. They fill bags with broken glass. They hammer long rusty nails through table legs to make spiked clubs.

When they see their arsenal laid out in front of them, they all nod their heads in satisfaction.

"This has to be enough to take them down," Nora says.

"It's at least enough to hurt them," Trish says.

Nora doesn't actually want to fight them up close. The spiked clubs are just in case they get into the treehouse, but her plan isn't to fight them head-on. She wants to focus on knocking them to the ground. When Mason told her about how traumatizing it was for him to be pushed out of the treehouse, Nora realized that's her best weapon. She wants to make them fall like Mason did. She wants to traumatize them to the point where they'll never want to climb up the tree ever again. That's why the most important weapons they have in their arsenal are the rocks. They're going to throw rocks at any one of them that climbs too high. When Nora tells them her strategy, they're in complete agreement. They each pick up a stone and smack them together like battle axes.

"Let's kick some goblin ass!" Trish cries.

Then they run out on the balcony, rushing into battle.

Once they get outside, they scream a battle cry and start throwing rocks at the goblins below. The little creatures are climbing up the trunk, dangling from branches, riding the tire swings. They have no idea what's coming for them. But as the children throw rocks at goblins, they realize that their plan has a big flaw in it. None of them have very good aim. They throw a dozen rocks at the climbing goblins, running back and forth to grab more, but not a single one hits a target.

"They're too heavy," Nora says. "We need smaller rocks."

Trish and Mason rush inside and get as many small rocks as they can. It's a good thing that rocks are considered goblin toys. They're able to get any rocks they want in any size and shape. There's no way that rocks can be broken or flawed, so they're able to get the strongest and most perfect throwing rocks imaginable.

Once they get stones with the right weight and size, they're able to throw more accurately. It's still not very easy to hit their target, but it's not impossible. They take five buckets full of rocks to the balcony and throw a barrage of missiles at the closest goblin, a small one hanging from a branch. It takes a dozen throws from each of them, but they finally get him a few times. He doesn't fall until Trish hits him right in the head and he loses his grip. The goblin lets out a skin-curdling scream as it drops and breaks both of its legs.

The three children look down at their victory, watching

the goblin crying in pain. Nora's never heard the voice of a goblin before. She didn't even know they were able to speak. The thing's cries are loud and shrill. Nora almost feels bad for the thing. It was once a child, even younger than her. But even though she knows she's responsible for the creature's suffering, she can't help but grow a smile on her face.

"We did it!" Nora cries in excitement.

"He's screaming!" Trish says, even more happy about it than Nora. "We actually hurt him!"

It gives them the confidence to continue. They know they can do it if they keep trying. Mason goes in and fills more buckets with rocks for them as the two girls try to knock more goblins out of the trees. They hit two more and send them spiraling into a world of pain without much effort at all. Once Nora gets the hang of it, she's able to throw the stones with such force and aim that she can peg any one of the disgusting creatures that come into her range.

But once there are a dozen of them on the ground writhing in pain, it sends the remaining goblins into a frenzy. They look up at the children with blood in their eyes. They want revenge. They want to cause the children the same pain they've caused their brethren. Although Nora never saw them as menacing—just a bunch of sad lost souls—she now understands they're not incapable of wrath. They rush the tree, climbing like a horde of mad berserkers. And they will not rest until all three children are punished for what they have done.

CHAPTER
EIGHT

℮

The goblins swarm the treehouse, screaming like a choir of demonic locusts. Their cries are so loud that Mason can hardly hear Nora as she barks orders at him. She tells him to materialize buckets full of rocks rather than getting them one at a time. Then Trish and Nora dump the buckets over the railing, showering the goblins with stones. They don't need good aim or throwing ability. Just a single bucket pour can take out two or three goblins at a time. The goblins scream as rocks rain down on them, grabbing at leaves and branches on the way down.

But there are still too many of them. Some of them are good at gripping onto the tree and don't fall no matter how many rocks hit them on the head. Others have gotten so high up into the tree that their rocks won't reach them. It doesn't take long before goblins are climbing over the railing and attacking the children head-on. Trish and Nora switch to the spiked clubs and swing at the goblins, trying to knock them off.

Up close, the goblins are more horrific than Nora

imagined. Their skin is like that of lizards. Their hair is matted and full of feathers and horns. They have long fangs and beady rat-like eyes. They foam at the mouth and growl like animals. There's no humanity left in them whatsoever.

When Nora swings a club into the skull of a goblin climbing over the railing toward her, the nails pierce its flesh and spray foul white liquid at her. It's not enough to knock the thing off. It grips the railing and screams in pain. Nora can't get the club out of its head, but she pulls and twists on it until the goblin is in so much pain that it crawls back down on its own, trying to escape the mad little girl before she can grab another club and hit him again. It makes her feel like her plan is working. She swings at the other goblins, not to knock them off but to cut them on the rusty nails and mangle their putrid flesh. She connects with one of them on the side of their face and rips open its cheek, gouging out an eyeball. It screams and recoils.

When she remembers her goal is not to knock them off but to hurt them so much they run away, she is able to relax and not panic so much. All they are doing is lining up to be hurt by her. They only make it easier by getting in range of her weapon.

Trish and Mason follow Nora's lead and begin fighting the goblins with the intent of causing pain both physically and psychologically. They use clubs and spears to aim for their faces, their eyes, and their legs, maiming or crippling them. Even though there are dozens of goblins climbing onto the balcony, the children keep them back by showing what will happen to them if they come too close. It doesn't take long before the goblins retreat. They pick up their wounded and run away, climbing down from the treehouse in a panic.

"We did it!" Mason cries. "We scared away the goblins!"

"We fucked them up!" Trish yells.

They shout and cheer as the goblins run away, throwing rocks and spears down at them, smiling so bright and filled with more hope than ever before. Nora isn't sure if it's just her imagination or not, but the two children are looking more human than ever before. Their goblin features appear to be receding. It's like this has given them enough optimism to fill them with positive energy. It might just be enough to save them from becoming goblins.

But before they have a chance to celebrate too much, Nora looks at them with a serious face and says, "It's not over yet."

The goblins are returning. This time they come with weapons. They carry spears and spiked clubs identical to the ones the children were using against them. Even the injured ones come back with a fury, wanting to inflict the same amount of pain on Nora that she inflicted on them.

Nora turns to Mason. "Get the grog."

Mason looks at her with confusion. "What? Why?"

"Just get it. Get as many cups of it as you can."

When he runs inside, she turns to Trish. "Get a bunch of rags from the toy box."

"What for?" Trish asks. "We should be making more clubs and buckets of rocks."

Nora shakes her head. "The grog is basically gasoline. If it ignites, we can make Molotov cocktails."

Trish doesn't have to question her any further. She runs inside to make rags and more earwax candles as well. Nora's seen how they are made on television many times before. She knows that if they really want to cause the goblins pain, they'll need to burn them alive. And because they have the high ground, the goblins won't have any way to fight back, even if they do come armed to the teeth in numbers twenty times larger than the trio.

When the molotovs are complete, the children line them up along the railing. Nora lights one of them, putting the candle right into the fluid and it ignites just as she predicted. The fluid is definitely flammable. It will work perfectly.

As the goblins storm the tree, the three children toss their burning cocktails down at them. The first one they throw hits a goblin right in the face and lights him on fire. The goblin falls to the ground screaming as the flames engulf him. The next several cocktails they throw miss their targets but create a barrier of fire between the goblins and the tree. Any of the creatures who pass over the flames do not get through unscathed. Many of them get the flammable liquid on their legs and feet, they climb up the tree with fire clinging to their clothing.

"It's working!" Nora cries. "Keep at it!"

They throw more and more of the cocktails. Several of the goblins are hit and catch on fire. They swing their clubs at the flames but it's not enough to put them out. It only catches their weapons on fire and spreads the flames. Mason goes inside and brings out grog by the bucketful. They don't even need to light it on fire anymore. They just dump the flammable liquid and drench the goblins with it, allowing the creatures to catch themselves on fire.

The goblins shriek in pain. They roll around, trying to get the fire off. Many of them stop moving as they are swallowed by the flames, either losing consciousness or just giving up and accepting their fate. As Nora watches them burn, listening to their pathetic cries, a smile creeps onto her face. She can't help but enjoy the suffering she's causing them. They deserve every second of pain for coming after them. And since they cannot die, their agony is only extended longer. They do not have the luxury of the sweet release of death.

But it's not just Nora who delights in their anguish. Both Mason and Trish are smiling and laughing as they burn the goblins up. A few of the creatures make it to them, climbing onto the balcony, screaming in pain as they are covered in fire. When they get close, Mason throws a bucket of grog at them to completely cover them with fire. Trish clubs them a few times, knocking them back. It doesn't take much before the goblins are jumping over the railing themselves, choosing to fall to the ground and break all their bones instead of facing the wild children for another moment.

As all the goblins burn, the children cheer in triumph. They can tell the creatures have had enough. The goblins no longer try to get up to them. They throw down their weapons and run away. Those who are on fire just continue rolling on the ground to put out the flames. They no longer care about the children in the treehouse. They don't want to have anything to do with any of them ever again.

"We did it!" Nora cries.

Mason hops up and down, yelling "They're running away!"

Trish continues tossing the last of her molotovs and says, "There's no way they'll mess with us ever again."

When Nora looks at the other children, she sees all of their goblin parts fading away completely. They become normal children again. The goblins have given up on all three of them. Although Nora was only focused on saving herself, she managed to help the other kids as well. Now they all can continue as human beings without having to join the goblin ranks. They have found a way to be sources of positive energy for the universe. Nora couldn't be happier with the outcome.

But before they have a chance to celebrate, she notices the fire spreading. It climbs up the tree and spreads to the forest around them. It brightens the sky with orange light. Mason kicks over an earwax candle and ignites the puddles of grog at their feet, spreading the fire even faster. The treehouse is made of old, dead wood that burns like kindling. It isn't long before the whole balcony is aflame.

When the children run to the back of the tree, they see the way down has been completely covered in a pool of fire. There's nowhere for them to escape. Smoke fills the air. The sound of crackling burning wood drowns out the screams of the remaining goblins. The children look around in a panic.

"We have to get higher," Nora says.

She knows there's no use if the fire keeps spreading, but it's the only option she can think of. If she goes down, she'll burn to death. Going up will at least buy her some time.

"This way," Trish yells, leading the younger children through the fire to climb higher.

It only takes a minute for the main section of the treehouse to go up in flames. They climb up to the bunk room, coughing on the smoke that fills the air. But once they go as far up in the tree as they've ever gone, Trish and Mason stop in their tracks. It's obvious to Nora that they are afraid to go higher.

"We can't go up there," Mason says. "The grim lurker will get us."

Trish won't admit it, but she looks just as worried about it as Mason.

Nora takes them to the edge of the platform, as far from the smoke as they can get and says, "The grim lurker is just a story. You don't know that he's actually real."

"But what if he is?" Mason asks. "The grim lurker is going to be angry at us for setting his home on fire."

"Would you rather wait here and get burned up? We should just keep going. I'm sure the story is just a fairy tale."

Mason looks down at the raging fire but doesn't respond. It's clear that he believes the story and is too scared to continue.

"Why bother going higher?" Trish asks. "The fire will catch up to us eventually."

"Will anyone come to rescue us if they see the fire?" Nora asks. "If we can just hold out until help arrives, I'm sure we'll be fine."

Trish shakes her head. "No one will come. There are no firefighters in Heaven."

Nora doesn't know what to do. She wonders if she should just jump out of the tree and hope that she survives. She'd break both of her legs but at least she would live. Looking down over the edge, she realizes that the chances of survival would be slim. Even if she survived the fall, the fire down there is growing out of control. It won't be long before the entire forest is ablaze. She wonders if her mother and grandmother will see the fire from a distance and come for her. She wonders if there's anything they can do to stop it. Her grandmother might know others who could help. It's unlikely but it might be the only chance she has.

"It's your call," Trish says. "We're already dead so it doesn't matter to us. We can burn up in the fire and be fine by tomorrow. But you've got a lot more to lose than us. If you make it, you can still grow up and have a life. You don't need to die."

Nora looks up at the rickety structures higher in the tree. She doesn't have much faith in her family rescuing her, but she decides that holding onto hope is her best solution. She's not in a rush to die. If she can stay alive for as long as possible there might just be a chance that luck will be on her side.

They continue climbing the tree to escape the flames. Trish and Nora are determined to make it, but Mason is still terrified. He only goes with them because he doesn't want to be left alone. His fear is getting the best of him. He's not just afraid of the grim lurker. The height is also overwhelming to him. When Nora looks back, she can tell his vertigo is preventing him from keeping up. She worries about the younger child but knows that he's not in as much danger as she is. She can't wait for him. She has to keep going.

But the higher they go, the more difficult it is for them to ascend. There aren't any stairs or ladders leading up to the structures above. They have no choice but to climb up the trunk of the tree, using branches as footholds.

"Keep going," Trish yells to them, leading the way up the tree.

Nora follows close behind, but Mason can't keep up. His fear is taking over and he doesn't have the strength to continue. By the time Nora gets ten branches higher, she doesn't realize that they've left Mason behind. He's wrapped around the trunk of the tree, tears flowing from his eyes. Even with the flames biting at his heels, he won't budge.

Trish yells down at him, "Come on, Mason! You can do it!"

But he doesn't answer. Mason just shivers and cries, gripping the tree even tighter. Before Trish yells at him again, he disappears into the smoke. They can only hear his screams as the flames reach him.

"Just keep going," Trish tells Nora. "He'll be fine."

Nora doesn't have time to worry about the boy. She continues her ascent, focusing on each branch at a time. They arrive at the closest structure and peer through the windows. It's dark and empty inside. It seems like it hasn't been visited in a hundred years.

But as they climb past it, Nora swears she can see a half-goblin face in the shadows, staring back at her. She doesn't give it a second thought, though. She keeps climbing, not interested in finding out whether it's real or just an illusion in the smoke.

But as they go higher, they pass more small treehouses and each one contains a different half-goblin watching their every move. She doesn't stop, though. She doesn't know if any of them are real. Trish doesn't seem to notice them, and Nora doesn't have time to ask her if they are actually there or just a hallucination. It's not until they get to the higher rooms, the ones that are lit by candlelight, that Nora realizes that there really are more children hiding up here. She can tell that Trish notices them as well, but she doesn't want to stop for them. The sight only makes her climb higher.

"Keep going," Trish says. "We're almost at the top."

But the half-goblins appear angry that they are climbing so close to their homes. They yell out at the invaders and start throwing rocks at them, attempting to knock them out of the tree. It's like they haven't had visitors come up in the tree that high before and are terrified of the newcomers. They're trying to protect their territory. They might even think they are goblins who have come to take them away.

It's a surprise to Nora that there are actually children hiding this high up in the treehouse. Trish and Mason had no idea that there was anyone else up here because they never climbed this high before. Nora wonders what they've been doing up here for all this time. They must have been in hiding for years, hoping the goblins would go for the new arrivals that stay far below.

None of them appear to be hobgoblins like the

grim lurker, but it's possible that they are how the story perpetuated. Nora wonders if new arrivals to the treehouse once saw these half-goblins up here and were convinced they were horrible hobgoblins that must be avoided. Or maybe these children are the ones who invented the myth in the first place so that nobody would invade this area, keeping the upper treehouses a place of safety for them. Whatever the case, the half-goblin children don't want them there. Nora is not safe.

"Stop it!" Nora yells at the children. "We're just trying to escape the fire!"

But the half-goblins continue throwing rocks. They must be able to materialize as many as they want from their toy boxes, because they seem to have a limitless supply of them. One rock pegs Nora in the hip and another in her arm, but she holds back the pain and continues climbing.

"Please stop!" Nora cries. "We won't hurt you!"

The half-goblins don't let up. Her words only make them throw the rocks harder.

"Don't bother," Trish calls down to Nora. "They've probably been up here for ages. They've gone crazy. Just ignore them and keep going."

"But don't they know about the fire?" Nora yells up at her. "They should be climbing with us."

Trish picks up her pace and says, "I already told you, they're crazy. Just keep moving."

As Trish finishes speaking, a rock hits her in the face and she loses her grip on the trunk of the tree. She cries out as blood gushes from her right eye. Nora can see her arms thrashing, trying to catch herself. But the branch beneath her feet breaks and she falls. Nora watches the girl drop past her, screaming all the way down until she disappears into the flames below.

Now that she's alone, Nora feels her heart sink into her chest. She doesn't have time to mourn Mason and Trish. They are both already dead, anyway. No matter how traumatic the experience was for them, they'll be fine eventually. Nora, on the other hand, is in far more danger. She has to get through this if she hopes to survive. And now she has to do it all alone.

She keeps climbing the tree, being hit by rock after rock. But she doesn't lose her grip. She doesn't let them knock her out of the tree. When she gets high enough, the half-goblins are only able to hit her in the butt and in the legs. They aren't able to prevent her ascension. Although she's in pain and can already feel her wounds swelling and turning black and blue, she pushes herself to keep going all the way to the top of the tree.

CHAPTER
NINE

There is only one structure left up above. It's twice as large as all the other treehouses up that high, built around the top of the trunk of the tree like a lookout tower. The branches are thin and flimsy up here, hardly enough to hold Nora's weight. But she keeps climbing.

When she gets to the floor of the uppermost treehouse, she sees a dim light glowing from a hatch and climbs toward it. She doesn't know what will be on the other side but is prepared for anything. If another half-goblin is in there, waiting to pummel her with rocks, she knows she'll have to fight them off. She's ready to even beat it to death and throw its body out of the tree if that's what it takes. Even if it's the grim lurker, she's not afraid. She'll do whatever it takes to stay alive.

The fire is far below her. Even the smoke hasn't reached this high up. But she knows it's still coming. She knows the fire will get her eventually without some kind of miracle. But she's still alive. She still has hope.

When she crawls through the hatch up into the highest structure in the tree, she finds herself in a goblin bedroom that appears well lived in. There are toys and trash littered across the splintered wood floor. A table and a single chair are on one side of the room with the bed and a nightstand on the other. It appears to be deserted until a tall figure steps out from behind the trunk of the tree. A man who looks older than Nora's grandmother stares at her, a half-goblin face with big beady eyes and a long pointed nose. His mouth is wide open, breathing heavily, looking at her like he wants to strangle her for entering his domain without permission.

Nora looks around the room for a weapon but doesn't find anything useful. A toy truck, an empty goblet, a wooden spoon. None of them seem like they will work against such a large man.

"Are you the grim lurker?" Nora finds herself asking.

The large man doesn't reply to her question. Instead, he says, "People call me Big John. I like when people call me Big John."

Then a crooked smile appears on his face. He doesn't seem malicious at all. Even though he's so enormous and intimidating, Nora feels like she's not in any danger in his presence. He's just a big kid who's been alone for a very long time.

"Want some soup?" the half-hobgoblin asks. "Big John likes soup."

He goes to the fridge and pulls out a bubbling bowl of mush. Nora says she's not hungry, but he hands it to her anyway. She holds the cold gruel away from her face so that she doesn't have to smell it, but doesn't eat a single bite. A big smile appears on the man's face, and he nods at the bowl, telling her that it's good. Nora can't believe anyone could possibly enjoy goblin food, but this man seems to be completely satisfied with it. In fact, he seems completely content with everything he has in his treehouse.

"Big John has lots of toys," he says, pointing at the broken goblin toys scattered on the ground. "You can play with them if you want."

Nora nods. She doesn't know what to make of him. He's obviously been here for a very long time. She doesn't want to play with his toys, but she finds herself unable to stop him from handing her headless dolls and toy boats as she stands there shivering in his presence.

She doesn't know what else to say but, "Thank you for the toys, but I didn't come here to play."

Big John nods and gives her more toys. He piles them up in her arms until they start falling out onto the floor.

"Do you know what's going on down below?" Nora asks, trying to change the subject. "The tree is on fire. My friends have already burned up."

Big John looks at her with a confused face. He doesn't know what she's talking about. Nora puts the pile of toys on the bed and goes to the window. She points at the bright red landscape, trying to show him the danger that they're in.

"See," Nora says, showing him the view from the window. "The fire is spreading."

When the half-hobgoblin looks outside, he just smiles and ignores her words.

He says, "The sky is pretty today. Big John likes the colors."

"It looks that way because of the fire. When it spreads higher it will burn your whole house down. Aren't you worried?"

He just responds by saying, "Big John hopes it stays pretty all night long. Big John likes pretty things."

After staring out the window for awhile, Nora is convinced he can see the fire but just doesn't care about the danger. Even with the sound of crackling wood and smoke billowing up past his window, he just smiles and inhales the smell as though it's a pleasant experience for him. It's like so little happens in his life at the top of the tree that a little excitement only makes him happier. He doesn't care about the danger. He's just enjoying the view of the fire down below while it lasts. He's happy that something new is happening to break up the monotony of his existence.

"Let's play a game," he tells Nora. "Big John likes to play games."

Nora doesn't know what to do. She wants to convince him that they're in danger, but he doesn't seem to care one way or another.

"I'm not dead like you," Nora says. "If the fire reaches

this high, I'll die and never be able to go home again."

Big John looks at her with a sad face. Then he opens up her arms and gives her a big hug. She becomes encompassed by his sweat and body odor but finds herself hugging him back. He doesn't hold back and squeezes her tightly, genuinely filling her with his love.

He begins to cry against her shoulder and says, "Big John wants to go home, too. But Big John can't go home until he's a good boy again."

After he lets her go, Nora asks, "How long have you been here?"

"Big John stopped counting the days a long, long time ago." Then he changes the subject. "Let's play now. We have lots of toys and games that will make us happy. If we don't stay happy the bad kids will come and take us away."

He goes to his toys and sets them up on his dining table, so he can show her which toys are his favorite ones. He especially likes the rusty train car and a melted plastic airplane.

"But the fire is growing. We don't have time to play with toys."

Big John shakes his head. "Nora shouldn't worry about the fire. The fire makes Nora sad. Nora needs to stay happy like Big John."

Nora is shocked by his words. She says, "Wait... How do you know my name? I never told it to you."

Big John holds up his melted airplane and flies it across her face, making a whooshing noise with pursed lips. Then he says, "Big John knows everything that happens in the goblin tree. Big John's ears are good at hearing things from far away."

"So, you've heard everything that's been happening down there?" Nora asks. "Why didn't you come help us?"

He nods. "Big John hates when kids are sad in the goblin tree. Big John used to try to help the kids below, try to help them be happy and have fun playing with toys. But the kids are always afraid of Big John so Big John leaves them alone now. Nobody comes to see Big John except for Nora."

As he plays with his toy airplane, Nora can see the pain and loneliness in his half-hobgoblin face. She can tell he's been through so much over the years. He's still human and has been desperately trying to hold onto his humanity for so long, all by himself. Nora can't help but feel sorry for the large man.

Even though the fire is continuing to rage around them, spreading across the forest and burning up the treehouse, Nora finds herself giving in to Big John's request. She decides to play toys with him. There's nothing she can do about the fire except hope that somebody comes to rescue them, so she figures that she might as well spend her time playing with Big John. It's better than being worried and afraid.

Big John pretends that his airplane is a rescue craft searching for the baby doll that Nora holds in her hand.

He tells her that the doll is sinking in quicksand and the plane is trying to find her to save her. The plane circles overhead while Big John makes whooshing sounds, pretending that he's the one flying the plane while Nora is the doll who needs to be rescued.

"Don't worry. Big John will save Nora from sinking. Big John is the best rescuer because he has the best rescue plane."

Big John circles the make-believe quicksand.

"Help me! Help me! I'm sinking!" Nora says in a high-pitched voice, pretending to be the doll in trouble.

But all Big John does is fly around in circles and never rescues the doll. Nora has the doll sink deeper and deeper in the make-believe quicksand, but the plane never comes.

"Help me! Help me!"

When the doll is all the way submerged, Nora makes choking and gagging noises like she is suffocating. The plane never comes. Nora tilts the doll, showing that she's suffocated to death and died.

Big John stops moving the airplane and looks at the dead doll with a sad face.

"You didn't rescue me in time," Nora says, holding up the doll as though it has sunk to the bottom of the quicksand.

Big John's lips tremble and he lowers his plane to his hip. He has tears in his eyes, as though this all really happened.

"Big John was having so much fun flying that he forgot to save Nora. Big John feels bad for letting Nora down."

He looks at her with a frowning face and then says, "Nobody saved Big John when he was drowning, either."

He drops his plane on the table and sits down in a chair, covering his face with his hands.

"Big John knows what it's like to die alone. Big John swore he'd save everyone who was in danger, no matter what. Big John doesn't want anyone to have to die like he did."

Nora feels bad for pretending that her doll died. She didn't know he would take the game so seriously. She decides to lift the doll up and pretend that she's still alive, calling out for help again.

"Wait, she's not dead yet," Nora says. "She still needs help. You can still rescue her in time."

But Big John isn't falling for it. He shakes his head and says, "It's too late. Big John already failed. That's just Nora's ghost. She doesn't realize that she already died."

As he mopes in his chair, Nora tries to get him to play something else. She gets a checkerboard out and tries to play checkers with him, but he doesn't seem interested. She pulls some stuffed animals from a pile on the floor and asks him to play zoo with her, but he doesn't care anymore. He's just too sad to play anything at all.

The fire spreads higher. It gets to the point where Nora can feel the heat. Smoke fills the room, causing them to cough and wheeze. It won't be long before the half-hobgoblin's treehouse catches fire and they burn to death. But Big John doesn't move. He's so sad that he doesn't even care about how the smoke is making it hard for him to breathe.

Nora can't help but panic. She can see branches on fire out the window. The smoke is so thick that she has to hold the shirt of her goblin costume over her mouth to prevent her from inhaling it. It won't be long before the fire swallows them whole.

"This is it," Nora says. "The fire is here."

Big John looks up and finally notices how bad it's gotten. It's like he had no idea the fire was such a threat until now. He stands up from his chair, a worried expression on his face.

Nora looks at the door of the treehouse as it catches fire. It goes up in flames within seconds and she screams. She rushes to the back of the room, holding her costume over her mouth, terrified of what is about to happen to her. She looks out the window, wondering if she can climb higher, but there's nowhere to go. There are no branches she can reach, and even if she could the only place she can go to is the top of Big John's treehouse and even that would only buy her a few more minutes. This is it. She has nowhere else to go.

She looks at Big John with tears in her eyes and says, "I don't want to die."

When she says this, Big John fills with emotion. He goes to her and hugs her again, even tighter than he did before. He holds her face to his chest and pets her head like she's a cat.

"Nora shouldn't be sad," Big John says. "Nora has Big John. At least Nora won't die alone."

But this only makes Nora cry louder. She doesn't want to die at all. If she dies she'll be stuck in Heaven forever. She'll never be able to go home or see her friends or be with her family. Even though she hates her mom and hates her little brother and hates pretty much everything about being alive, she'd rather live than die. She knows that she'll be able to live her life to the fullest as long as she has the chance to go back to her world and live to appreciate what she has.

When the floor catches fire under their feet, Nora screams again. She tries to climb up the trunk of the tree in the middle of the room, but can't get a good grip. Big John just stares at her, standing in the flames as though he doesn't feel it.

As she slides down the trunk, her pants and her shoes catch fire. Big John grabs her and picks her up in his arms, cradling her like a baby. Nora calms down a little, but the smoke is getting so thick that she can barely breathe or see. She knows it will be only a minute or two before she'll suffocate to death on the smoke. She just sobs against his chest and waits for the inevitable.

But then Big John composes himself. He looks down at her and rubs the tears from her eyes.

"Nora shouldn't cry," he tells her. "Big John will save Nora. Big John promised to help people in trouble."

He kicks open the back wall of the treehouse and looks down below.

"Big John will give you a piggyback ride," he says.

Nora doesn't resist. She lets him throw her over his shoulder and wraps herself around his back.

"Hold tight," Big John says.

Then he jumps. Nora screams as they fall through the air, gripping him as tight as she can. They land on a branch below and it cracks under the weight. Before it falls, Big John jumps down into the flames. He lands on a treehouse balcony. Even though his legs and waist catch on fire, he doesn't cry out in pain. He just holds Nora away from the flames as he climbs over the railing and jumps again.

Nora can't pay attention to anything after that. The thick smoke overwhelms her, causing her to close her eyes tight and press her face against the half-hobgoblin's back. She drifts in and out of consciousness as Big John swings like a gorilla from branch to branch, climbing deeper into the flames. Although he is burned badly, he endures the pain, insistent on bringing the young girl to safety.

When they get to the ground, Big John races through the forest fire, passing burned-up goblins and other trees that have gone up in flames. He takes her as far as he can out of danger until he collapses on the ground, falling face-first into the dirt.

When Nora opens her eyes and comes to, she sees that they are safely out of danger. The forest fire has barely spread to the area where they lie. She climbs off of Big John's back and gets to her feet, noticing the state of the half-hobgoblin. His legs are charred like burnt wood. His arms and face are black with soot. If he was a living person, he would have died from these wounds.

But Big John is already dead, so he won't die. The wounds will heal. He's still in incredible pain, however, and Nora feels horrible that he had to go through so much because of her. She doesn't know how to thank him for all he's done.

"Come on," Nora says, trying to pick him up off the ground. "We're not out of the forest yet."

But she can't lift the large man. He coughs and wheezes, gripping at the pain in his legs.

"Nora should keep going," he tells her. "Nora isn't safe yet."

When he says this, she sees that the fire is still spreading. The wind is blowing it in their direction. She has to keep moving. She has to leave her large friend behind.

She tugs on him and says, "You can't stay here. You'll be burned up."

Big John tries to get to his feet but just falls back into the dirt. His legs are crumbling as though they are more ash than flesh. There's no way he can move on his own and no way Nora can move him by herself. She has no choice but to leave him behind.

As she tells Big John goodbye, he looks up at her with a smile on his face, tears in his eyes. His hobgoblin parts have faded from his body and Nora can see what he looked like when he was human. Even though he was an adult, he has such a childlike look to his face. He looks like just a young innocent boy, much younger than Nora or even her little brother. Tears flow from his eyes as he looks at her. Then he turns away, rolling onto his back to see the flames they left behind.

"The forest is so pretty like this, isn't it?" he asks. "Big John likes the pretty colors."

Nora nods and wipes away her tears.

She says, "I have to go now."

But Big John doesn't mind. He waves at her and says, "It's okay. Nora doesn't have to worry about Big John. Big John wants to stay and watch the pretty colors for a bit longer."

Nora gives him a last hug goodbye and then leaves him lying in the forest. She rushes away, only looking back once to see if he's okay. The fire keeps growing and it isn't long before he's swallowed by the smoke and flames. There aren't any screams or cries of agony. He just disappears into the fire as Nora runs to safety.

CHAPTER TEN

Nora waits on the side of the road for several hours until her mom and grandmother come to pick her up. They seem surprised to see her, like they had no faith that she had any chance of surviving the goblin treehouse. Even Nora's grandmother who filled her with confidence is astonished when she discovers Nora standing on the side of the road, waving their car over.

"What the hell did you do to your clothes?" Nora's mother says, complaining about all the ash and soot covering her daughter's outfit.

Of course, the first thing she has to say to her is criticism, rather than relief that she's alright. She doesn't even seem concerned about the fire in the distance that Nora had just barely survived.

"You're not getting all that stuff in *my* car," her mother says.

But Nora opens the car door and sits in the back seat anyway, rubbing her blackened backside into the upholstery just to piss her off.

"What did I just say!" her mother screams.

Nora rolls her eyes and says, "Just drive."

Her mother huffs and pouts as she puts her car in gear and drives them back toward the grandmother's dwelling.

"You're so grounded when we get home," her mother says.

Nora just laughs at her and says, "Whatever."

She hoped her family would have been happier to see her. She thought she was going to die back there and is surprised she survived at all. Even her grandmother doesn't seem to care about what happened to her back in the treehouse. It makes Nora wonder if Trish was right, that her grandmother actually was trying to sacrifice her granddaughter to the goblins so that she'd get a better piece of Heaven in her afterlife. But Nora decides not to worry about it. If her grandmother really wanted that then she's just a miserable old lady who doesn't deserve her love or attention ever again.

They spend the rest of the weekend doing boring family stuff that Nora doesn't want anything to do with. She spends the whole trip in her room drawing pictures, staring out the window at the forest in the distance. She wonders what happened to Trish and Mason and even Big John. She hopes they're all alright now. She hopes they have been able to leave the treehouse and go to their own domains. She doesn't want any of them to become goblins after what they all went through together. She wants them all to find eternal happiness.

When Nora returns home, everything goes back to the way it used to be. She still has to deal with her nagging mother and annoying brother. She still cuts mohawks into her Barbie dolls because she thinks normal dolls are boring and ugly the way they're supposed to be. At school, she thinks all of her friends are assholes and all of the teachers are stupid. She has tried telling everyone about the goblins in Heaven and how they're going to become one of them if they die miserable while they're still kids. But nobody believes her. Their parents never told any of them about the goblins. She thinks it's so dangerous that nobody knows about them. If she knew she never would have been taken to the treehouse. She never would have been sacrificed as she was.

But she knows that she can't be negative forever. She has to stay positive. If she hopes to go to Heaven after she dies, she can't be such a spiteful, hateful child. She can't go to Hell. She can't become a goblin. She has to live for her own personal happiness, even if it means making all the people around her miserable.

The next time they are supposed to go to Heaven to visit their grandmother, Nora refuses to go. The last trip was so traumatic for her that she doesn't want to go again. She says she'll only go if she can visit her friends Trish, Mason, and Big John. She doesn't care about her grandmother. She just wants to know if her friends are doing alright. But because she doesn't know where to find them, doesn't even know their last names, there's no way for her to figure out which domain to visit them in. They could have all become goblins by now for all she knows. She decides it would be for the best not to know for sure. She decides she would prefer to imagine that they made it out of the treehouse and became sources of positive energy like the other citizens of Heaven, not because she's convinced it's the truth but because it makes her happy imagining that's what happened to them. And it's more important to her to be happy than to know the truth.

No matter what her parents do, no matter how much they threaten her, there's no way they are ever able to get her to go to Heaven ever again. Her father has to stay with her whenever the family goes to Heaven to visit their grandmother until she's old enough to stay home on her own. They've tried bribing her and convincing her how much her grandmother misses her, but she refuses to go.

She spends her whole life doing only the things that make her happy. She gets a job in graphic design because it's the only thing she can do that she enjoys that can bring in enough money to keep her positive. She only dates guys who give her whatever she wants. She has no guilt over leaving men who don't put her needs above their own. She has no problem screwing over friends or strangers or even family members if it means that she can get just a little bit more happiness in her life. She's fine being the worst human being who's ever walked the earth as long as she can get into Heaven, because she knows the universe doesn't care about who's good or who's evil. The universe is a selfish thing that only cares about being fed the exact type of energy it needs in order to continue for all of eternity. Nora has long since accepted this fact and knows exactly how to live to stay as positive as she needs to be.

But it's not long before everyone else in the world figures this out as well. In a single generation after the gateway to Heaven was invented, people stop caring about doing good for others and only care about their own happiness. They're all so obsessed with the idea of becoming positive sources of energy for the universe that they lose all sense of what it really means to help people in need. The only people who help others are those who get happiness out of the act, which is just barely enough for the misfortunate to get by. And it's not like the world has changed for the worse. It's exactly the same as it's always been. People have always been focused solely on their own needs and for some reason it's always worked to keep the human race on track.

And years later when Nora is on her deathbed, an old lady who never had children to continue her legacy, never had any real friends who she cared about enough to leave any meaningful impression on their lives, she wonders if her happiness ever really meant anything to anyone but her. She wonders if going to Heaven was worth all the misery she caused to all the people around her. But instead of dying with regrets, she fades away with a big smile on her face. Because she knows that in the end, all those other people don't matter. All she needs is her eternal bliss and everyone else can go the fuck to hell.

BONUS SECTION

This is the part of the book where we would have published an afterword by the author but he insisted on drawing a comic strip instead for reasons we don't quite understand.

Thanks for reading my newest book, Goblins on the Other Side. Wasn't it gobliny?

It's me CM3!

Like my books *Ugly Heaven, Punk Land,* and *The Boy with the Chainsaw Heart,* this book is set in the afterlife.

Ever since I was a kid, I've been fascinated by the concept of a world after we die. I was obsessed with imagining what it could possibly be like. Would it be Heaven and Hell like my parents told me? Or would it be something far more interesting and fantastical?

Is it *What Dreams May Come?* Or is it more like *Beetlejuice?*

No offense to Christians, but I've always thought the idea of going to Heaven after you die was kind of cheap and lame. I guess it's better than Hell, but still... way too bland and unimaginative.

So I like imagining alternatives to Heaven. Like the punk rock afterlife of *Punk Land* or the grotesque dreamscape of *Ugly Heaven.*

I have a friend who believes that the afterlife is different for everyone.

She thinks that whatever you believe the afterlife will be is exactly what it will be after you die.

If this is true, then I guess if you believe you will go to Heaven when you die then you'll end up in your ideal version of Heaven. And if you think you deserve to go to Hell then you're going to suffer in Hell.

And if you think you're going to battle frost giants in Valhalla then you'll battle frost giants in Valhalla.

This isn't another panel. There's just a tiny clone of me that follows me around and finishes my sentences.

But if the afterlife will be whatever you believe it will be, then there's a part of me that wants to start believing in completely ridiculous versions of the afterlife just in case.

Like maybe I can convince myself that we all turn into giant hotdogs with chainsaw arms once we die and fight each other for supremacy in a giant gladiator arena for all eternity.

THE
END

ABOUT THE AUTHOR

Carlton Mellick III is one of the leading authors of the bizarro fiction subgenre. Since 2001, his books have drawn an international cult following, despite the fact that they have been shunned by most libraries and chain bookstores.

He won the Wonderland Book Award for his novel, *Warrior Wolf Women of the Wasteland*, in 2009. His short fiction has appeared in *Vice Magazine, The Year's Best Fantasy and Horror #16, The Magazine of Bizarro Fiction*, and *Zombies: Encounters with the Hungry Dead*, among others. He is also a graduate of Clarion West, where he studied under the likes of Chuck Palahniuk, Connie Willis, and Cory Doctorow.

He lives in Portland, OR, the bizarro fiction mecca.

Visit him online at **www.carltonmellick.com**

QUICKSAND HOUSE

Tick and Polly have never met their parents before. They live in the same house with them, they dream about them every night, they share the same flesh and blood, yet for some reason their parents have never found the time to visit them even once since they were born. Living in a dark corner of their parents' vast crumbling mansion, the children long for the day when they will finally be held in their mother's loving arms for the first time... But that day seems to never come. They worry their parents have long since forgotten about them.

When the machines that provide them with food and water stop functioning, the children are forced to venture out of the nursery to find their parents on their own. But the rest of the house is much larger and stranger than they ever could have imagined. The maze-like hallways are dark and seem to go on forever, deranged creatures lurk in every shadow, and the bodies of long-dead children litter the abandoned storerooms. Every minute out of the nursery is a constant battle for survival. And the deeper into the house they go, the more they must unravel the mysteries surrounding their past and the world they've grown up in, if they ever hope to meet the parents they've always longed to see.

Like a survival horror rendition of *Flowers in the Attic*, Carlton Mellick III's *Quicksand House* is his most gripping and sincere work to date.

HUNGRY BUG

In a world where magic exists, spell-casting has become a serious addiction. It ruins lives, tears families apart, and eats away at the fabric of society. Those who cast too much are taken from our world, never to be heard from again. They are sent to a realm known as Hell's Bottom—a sorcerer ghetto where everyday life is a harsh struggle for survival. Porcelain dolls crawl through the alleys like rats, arcane scientists abduct people from the streets to use in their ungodly experiments, and everyone lives in fear of the aristocratic race of spider people who prey on citizens like vampires.

Told in a series of interconnected stories reminiscent of Frank Miller's *Sin City* and David Lapham's *Stray Bullets*, Carlton Mellick III's *Hungry Bug* is an urban fairy tale that focuses on the real life problems that arise within a fantastic world of magic.

STACKING DOLL

Benjamin never thought he'd ever fall in love with anyone, let alone a Matryoshkan, but from the moment he met Ynaria he knew she was the only one for him. Although relationships between humans and Matryoshkans are practically unheard of, the two are determined to get married despite objections from their friends and family. After meeting Ynaria's strict conservative parents, it becomes clear to Benjamin that the only way they will approve of their union is if they undergo The Trial—a matryoshkan wedding tradition where couples lock themselves in a house for several days in order to introduce each other to all of the people living inside of them.

SNUGGLE CLUB

After the death of his wife, Ray Parker decides to get involved with the local "cuddle party" community in order to once again feel the closeness of another human being. Although he's sure it will be a strange and awkward experience, he's determined to give anything a try if it will help him overcome his crippling loneliness. But he has no idea just how unsettling of an experience it will be until it's far too late to escape.

MOUSE TRAP

It's the last school trip young Emily will ever get to go on. Not because it's the end of the school year, but because the world is coming to an end. Teachers, parents, and other students have been slowly dying off over the past several months, killed in mysterious traps that have been appearing across the countryside. Nobody knows where the traps come from or who put them there, but they seem to be designed to exterminate the entirety of the human race.

Emily thought it was going to be an ordinary trip to the local amusement park, but what was supposed to be a normal afternoon of bumper cars and roller coasters has turned into a fight for survival after their teacher is horrifically killed in front of them, leaving the small children to fend for themselves in a life or death game of mouse and mouse trap.

NEVERDAY

Karl Lybeck has been repeating the same day over and over again, in a constant loop, for what feels like a thousand years. He thought he was the only person trapped in this eternal hell until he meets a young woman named January who is trapped in the same loop that Karl's been stuck within for so many centuries. But it turns out that Karl and January aren't alone. In fact, the majority of the population has been repeating the same day just as they have been. And society has mutated into something completely different from the world they once knew.

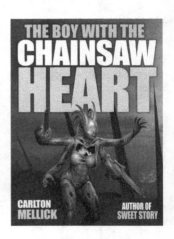

THE BOY WITH THE CHAINSAW HEART

Mark Knight awakens in the afterlife and discovers that he's been drafted into Hell's army, forced to fight against the hordes of murderous angels attacking from the North. He finds himself to be both the pilot and the fuel of a demonic war machine known as Lynx, a living demon woman with the ability to mutate into a weaponized battle suit that reflects the unique destructive force of a man's soul.

PARASITE MILK

Irving Rice has just arrived on the planet Kynaria to film an episode of the popular Travel Channel television series *Bizarre Foods with Andrew Zimmern: Intergalactic Edition.* Having never left his home state, let alone his home planet, Irving is hit with a severe case of culture shock. He's not prepared for Kynaria's mushroom cities, fungus-like citizens, or the giant insect wildlife. He's also not prepared for the consequences after he spends the night with a beautiful nymph-like alien woman who infects Irving with dangerous sexually-transmitted parasites that turn his otherworldly business trip into an agonizing fight for survival.

THE BIG MEAT

In the center of the city once known as Portland, Oregon, there lies a mountain of flesh. Hundreds of thousands of tons of rotting flesh. It has filled the city with disease and dead-lizard stench, contaminated the water supply with its greasy putrid fluids, clogged the air with toxic gasses so thick that you can't leave your house without the aid of a gas mask. And no one really knows quite what to do about it. A thousand-man demolition crew has been trying to clear it out one piece at a time, but after three months of work they've barely made a dent. And then there's the junkies who have started burrowing into the monster's guts, searching for a drug produced by its fire glands, setting back the excavation even longer.

It seems like the corpse will never go away. And with the quarantine still in place, we're not even allowed to leave. We're stuck in this disgusting rotten hell forever.

THE TERRIBLE THING THAT HAPPENS

There is a grocery store. The last grocery store in the world. It stands alone in the middle of a vast wasteland that was once our world. The open sign is still illuminated, brightening the black landscape. It can be seen from miles away, even through the poisonous red ash. Every night at the exact same time, the store comes alive. It becomes exactly as it was before the world ended. Its shelves are replenished with fresh food and water. Ghostly shoppers walk the aisles. The scent of freshly baked breads can be smelled from the rust-caked parking lot. For generations, a small community of survivors, hideously mutated from the toxic atmosphere, have survived by collecting goods from the store. But it is not an easy task. Decades ago, before the world was destroyed, there was a terrible thing that happened in this place. A group of armed men in brown paper masks descended on the shopping center, massacring everyone in sight. This horrible event reoccurs every night, in the exact same manner. And the only way the wastelanders can gather enough food for their survival is to traverse the killing spree, memorize the patterns, and pray they can escape the bloodbath in tact.

BIO MELT

Nobody goes into the Wire District anymore. The place is an industrial wasteland of poisonous gas clouds and lakes of toxic sludge. The machines are still running, the drone-operated factories are still spewing biochemical fumes over the city, but the place has lain abandoned for decades.

When the area becomes flooded by a mysterious black ooze, six strangers find themselves trapped in the Wire District with no chance of escape or rescue.

EVER TIME WE MEET AT THE DAIRY QUEEN, YOUR WHOLE FUCKING FACE EXPLODES

Ethan is in love with the weird girl in school. The one with the twitchy eyes and spiders in her hair. The one who can't sit still for even a minute and speaks in an odd squeaky voice. The one they call Spiderweb.

Although she scares all the other kids in school, Ethan thinks Spiderweb is the cutest, sweetest, most perfect girl in the world. But there's a problem. Whenever they go on a date at the Dairy Queen, her whole fucking face explodes.

EXERCISE BIKE

There is something wrong with Tori Manetti's new exercise bike. It is made from flesh and bone. It eats and breathes and poops. It was once a billionaire named Darren Oscarson who underwent years of cosmetic surgery to be transformed into a human exercise bike so that he could live out his deepest sexual fantasy. Now Tori is forced to ride him, use him as a normal piece of exercise equipment, no matter how grotesque his appearance.

SPIDER BUNNY

Only Petey remembers the Fruit Fun cereal commercials of the 1980s. He remembers how warped and disturbing they were. He remembers the lumpy-shaped cartoon children sitting around a breakfast table, eating puffy pink cereal brought to them by the distortedly animated mascot, Berry Bunny. The characters were creepier than the Sesame Street Humpty Dumpty, freakier than Mr. Noseybonk from the old BBC show Jigsaw. They used to give him nightmares as a child. Nightmares where Berry Bunny would reach out of the television and grab him, pulling him into her cereal bowl to be eaten by the demented cartoon children.

When Petey brings up Fruit Fun to his friends, none of them have any idea what he's talking about. They've never heard of the cereal or seen the commercials before. And they're not the only ones. Nobody has ever heard of it. There's not even any information about Fruit Fun on google or wikipedia. At first, Petey thinks he's going crazy. He wonders if all of those commercials were real or just false memories. But then he starts seeing them again. Berry Bunny appears on his television, promoting Fruit Fun cereal in her squeaky unsettling voice. And the next thing Petey knows, he and his friends are sucked into the cereal commercial and forced to survive in a surreal world populated by cartoon characters made flesh.

SWEET STORY

Sally is an odd little girl. It's not because she dresses as if she's from the Edwardian era or spends most of her time playing with creepy talking dolls. It's because she chases rainbows as if they were butterflies. She believes that if she finds the end of the rainbow then magical things will happen to her--leprechauns will shower her with gold and fairies will grant her every wish. But when she actually does find the end of a rainbow one day, and is given the opportunity to wish for whatever she wants, Sally asks for something that she believes will bring joy to children all over the world. She wishes that it would rain candy forever. She had no idea that her innocent wish would lead to the extinction of all life on earth.

TUMOR FRUIT

Eight desperate castaways find themselves stranded on a mysterious deserted island. They are surrounded by poisonous blue plants and an ocean made of acid. Ravenous creatures lurk in the toxic jungle. The ghostly sound of crying babies can be heard on the wind.

Once they realize the rescue ships aren't coming, the eight castaways must band together in order to survive in this inhospitable environment. But survival might not be possible. The air they breathe is lethal, there is no shelter from the elements, and the only food they have to consume is the colorful squid-shaped tumors that grow from a mentally disturbed woman's body.

AS SHE STABBED ME GENTLY IN THE FACE

Oksana Maslovskiy is an award-winning artist, an internationally adored fashion model, and one of the most infamous serial killers this country has ever known. She enjoys murdering pretty young men with a nine-inch blade, cutting them open and admiring their delicate insides. It's the only way she knows how to be intimate with another human being. But one day she meets a victim who cannot be killed. His name is Gabriel—a mysterious immortal being with a deep desire to save Oksana's soul. He makes her a deal: if she promises to never kill another person again, he'll become her eternal murder victim.

What at first seems like the perfect relationship for Oksana quickly devolves into a living nightmare when she discovers that Gabriel enjoys being killed by her just a little too much. He turns out to be obsessive, possessive, and paranoid that she might be murdering other men behind his back. And because he is unkillable, it's not going to be easy for Oksana to get rid of him.

CUDDLY HOLOCAUST

Teddy bears, dollies, and little green soldiers—they've all had enough of you. They're sick of being treated like playthings for spoiled little brats. They have no rights, no property, no hope for a future of any kind. You've left them with no other option-in order to be free, they must exterminate the human race.

Julie is a human girl undergoing reconstructive surgery in order to become a stuffed animal. Her plan: to infiltrate enemy lines in order to save her family from the toy death camps. But when an army of plushy soldiers invade the underground bunker where she has taken refuge, Julie will be forced to move forward with her plan despite her transformation being not entirely complete.

ARMADILLO FISTS

A weird-as-hell gangster story set in a world where people drive giant mechanical dinosaurs instead of cars.

Her name is Psycho June Howard, aka Armadillo Fists, a woman who replaced both of her hands with living armadillos. She was once the most bloodthirsty fighter in the world of illegal underground boxing. But now she is on the run from a group of psychotic gangsters who believe she's responsible for the death of their boss. With the help of a stegosaurus driver named Mr. Fast Awesome—who thinks he is God's gift to women even though he doesn't have any arms or legs--June must do whatever it takes to escape her pursuers, even if she has to kill each and every one of them in the process.

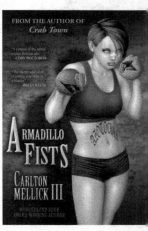

VILLAGE OF THE MERMAIDS

Mermaids are protected by the government under the Endangered Species Act, which means you aren't able to kill them even in self-defense. This is especially problematic if you happen to live in the isolated fishing village of Siren Cove, where there exists a healthy population of mermaids in the surrounding waters that view you as the main source of protein in their diet.

The only thing keeping these ravenous sea women at bay is the equally-dangerous supply of human livestock known as Food People. Normally, these "feeder humans" are enough to keep the mermaid population happy and well-fed. But in Siren Cove, the mermaids are avoiding the human livestock and have returned to hunting the frightened local fishermen. It is up to Doctor Black, an eccentric representative of the Food People Corporation, to investigate the matter and hopefully find a way to correct the mermaids' new eating patterns before the remaining villagers end up as fish food. But the more he digs, the more he discovers there are far stranger and more dangerous things than mermaids hidden in this ancient village by the sea.

I KNOCKED UP SATAN'S DAUGHTER

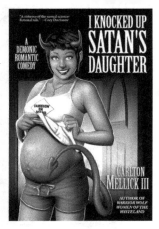

Jonathan Vandervoo lives a carefree life in a house made of legos, spending his days building lego sculptures and his nights getting drunk with his only friend—an alcoholic sumo wrestler named Shoji. It's a pleasant life with no responsibility, until the day he meets Lici. She's a soul-sucking demon from hell with red skin, glowing eyes, a forked tongue, and pointy red devil horns... and she claims to be nine months pregnant with Jonathan's baby.

Now Jonathan must do the right thing and marry the succubus or else her demonic family is going to rip his heart out through his ribcage and force him to endure the worst torture hell has to offer for the rest of eternity. But can Jonathan really love a fire-breathing, frog-eating, cold-blooded demoness? Or would eternal damnation be preferable? Either way, the big day is approaching. And once Jonathan's conservative Christian family learns their son is about to marry a spawn of Satan, it's going to be all-out war between demons and humans, with Jonathan and his hell-born bride caught in the middle.

KILL BALL

In a city where everyone lives inside of plastic bubbles, there is no such thing as intimacy. A husband can no longer kiss his wife. A mother can no longer hug her children. To do this would mean instant death. Ever since the disease swept across the globe, we have become isolated within our own personal plastic prison cells, rolling aimlessly through rubber streets in what are essentially man-sized hamster balls.

Colin Hinchcliff longs for the touch of another human being. He can't handle the loneliness, the confinement, and he's horribly claustrophobic. The only thing keeping him going is his unrequited love for an exotic dancer named Siren, a woman who has never seen his face, doesn't even know his name. But when The Kill Ball, a serial slasher in a black leather sphere, begins targeting women at Siren's club, Colin decides he has to do whatever it takes in order to protect her... even if he has to break out of his bubble and risk everything to do it.

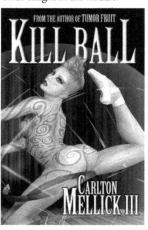

THE TICK PEOPLE

They call it Gloom Town, but that isn't its real name. It is a sad city, the saddest of cities, a place so utterly depressing that even their ales are brewed with the most sorrow-filled tears. They built it on the back of a colossal mountain-sized animal, where its woeful citizens live like human fleas within the hairy, pulsing landscape. And those tasked with keeping the city in a state of constant melancholy are the Stressmen-a team of professional sadness-makers who are perpetually striving to invent new ways of causing absolute misery.

But for the Stressman known as Fernando Mendez, creating grief hasn't been so easy as of late. His ideas aren't effective anymore. His treatments are more likely to induce happiness than sadness. And if he wants to get back in the game, he's going to have to relearn the true meaning of despair.

THE HAUNTED VAGINA

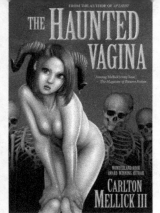

It's difficult to love a woman whose vagina is a gateway to the world of the dead...

Steve is madly in love with his eccentric girlfriend, Stacy. Unfortunately, their sex life has been suffering as of late, because Steve is worried about the odd noises that have been coming from Stacy's pubic region. She says that her vagina is haunted. She doesn't think it's that big of a deal. Steve, on the other hand, completely disagrees.

When a living corpse climbs out of her during an awkward night of sex, Stacy learns that her vagina is actually a doorway to another world. She persuades Steve to climb inside of her to explore this strange new place. But once inside, Steve finds it difficult to return... especially once he meets an oddly attractive woman named Fig, who lives within the lonely haunted world between Stacy's legs.

THE CANNIBALS OF CANDYLAND

There exists a race of cannibals who are made out of candy. They live in an underground world filled with lollipop forests and gumdrop goblins. During the day, while you are away at work, they come above ground and prowl our streets for food. Their prey: your children. They lure young boys and girls to them with their sweet scent and bright colorful candy coating, then rip them apart with razor sharp teeth and claws.

When he was a child, Franklin Pierce witnessed the death of his siblings at the hands of a candy woman with pink cotton candy hair. Since that day, the candy people have become his obsession. He has spent his entire life trying to prove that they exist. And after discovering the entrance to the underground world of the candy people, Franklin finds himself venturing into their sugary domain. His mission: capture one of them and bring it back, dead or alive.

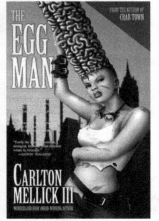

THE EGG MAN

It is a survival of the fittest world where humans reproduce like insects, children are the property of corporations, and having a ten-foot tall brain is a grotesque sexual fetish.

Lincoln has just been released into the world by the Georges Organization, a corporation that raises creative types. A Smell, he has little prospect of succeeding as a visual artist. But after he moves into the Henry Building, he meets Luci, the weird and grimy girl who lives across the hall. She is a Sight. She is also the most disgusting woman Lincoln has ever met. Little does he know, she will soon become his muse.

Now Luci's boyfriend is threatening to kill Lincoln, two rival corporations are preparing for war, and Luci is dragging him along to discover the truth about the mysterious egg man who lives next door. Only the strongest will survive in this tale of individuality, love, and mutilation.

APESHIT

Apeshit is Mellick's love letter to the great and terrible B-horror movie genre. Six trendy teenagers (three cheerleaders and three football players) go to an isolated cabin in the mountains for a weekend of drinking, partying, and crazy sex, only to find themselves in the middle of a life and death struggle against a horribly mutated psychotic freak that just won't stay dead. Mellick parodies this horror cliché and twists it into something deeper and stranger. It is the literary equivalent of a grindhouse film. It is a splatter punk's wet dream. It is perhaps one of the most fucked up books ever written.

If you are a fan of Takashi Miike, Evil Dead, early Peter Jackson, or Eurotrash horror, then you must read this book.

CLUSTERFUCK

A bunch of douchebag frat boys get trapped in a cave with subterranean cannibal mutants and try to survive not by using their wits but by following the bro code...

From master of bizarro fiction Carlton Mellick III, author of the international cult hits Satan Burger and Adolf in Wonderland, comes a violent and hilarious B movie in book form. Set in the same woods as Mellick's splatterpunk satire Apeshit, Clusterfuck follows Trent Chesterton, alpha bro, who has come up with what he thinks is a flawless plan to get laid. He invites three hot chicks and his three best bros on a weekend of extreme cave diving in a remote area known as Turtle Mountain, hoping to impress the ladies with his expert caving skills.

But things don't quite go as Trent planned. For starters, only one of the three chicks turns out to be remotely hot and she has no interest in him for some inexplicable reason. Then he ends up looking like a total dumbass when everyone learns he's never actually gone caving in his entire life. And to top it all off, he's the one to get blamed once they find themselves lost and trapped deep underground with no way to turn back and no possible chance of rescue. What's a bro to do? Sure he could win some points if he actually tried to save the ladies from the family of unkillable subterranean cannibal mutants hunting them for their flesh, but fuck that. No slam piece is worth that amount of effort. He'd much rather just use them as bait so that he can save himself.

THE BABY JESUS BUTT PLUG

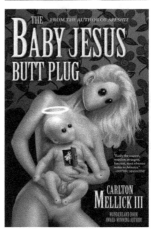

Step into a dark and absurd world where human beings are slaves to corporations, people are photocopied instead of born, and the baby jesus is a very popular anal probe.

CPSIA information can be obtained
at www.ICGtesting.com
Printed in the USA
LVHW022104110422
715897LV00005B/102